"I am *not* looking for a husband!"

A newspaper article to the contrary had a line of men snaked around her shop this morning.

When Jake grinned, she asked, "You find this amusing?"

"More like eye-opening. You're full of surprises today, Maggie."

"Am I? Normally I'm as uncomplicated as vanilla ice cream."

"I like vanilla ice cream." He leaned closer.

She pointed to the door. "Stand in line."

"You're not good for a man's ego."

Wait. Here she was discouraging Jake when she should be encouraging him. She mustered a smile. "Maybe you could help me… We're friends, so maybe we could do some things together."

"Wait a minute. Are you asking me out?"

"I need my life to return to normal. I want that line outside to go away. I want people to say 'Maggie who?'"

"This is Paradise. Good luck," he scoffed, then he stared at her. "I'll give your plan a shot if it'll help. Because when you're distracted, trouble follows."

Just then reality sneaked up on her. She would now be dating Jake MacLaughlin.

Could things get any worse?

Tina Radcliffe has been dreaming and scribbling for years. Originally from western New York, she left home for a tour of duty with the Army Security Agency stationed in Augsburg, Germany, and ended up in Tulsa, Oklahoma. Her past careers include certified oncology RN and library cataloger. She recently moved from Denver, Colorado, to the Phoenix, Arizona, area, where she writes heartwarming and fun inspirational romance.

Books by Tina Radcliffe

Love Inspired

The Rancher's Reunion
Oklahoma Reunion
Mending the Doctor's Heart
Stranded with the Rancher
Safe in the Fireman's Arms

Safe in the Fireman's Arms

Tina Radcliffe

ISBN-13: 978-0-373-81844-0

Safe in the Fireman's Arms

This edition published by arrangement with Love Inspired Books.

www.Harlequin.com

Printed in U.S.A.

Therefore there is now no condemnation
for those who are in Christ Jesus.
—*Romans* 8:1

Acknowledgments

It's always an honor to thank the very nice people who assist me with my writing from near and far, and this book was no exception.

Many thanks to Nancy Connally, the beta reader for the proposal of this book. Thank you to Joe and Jessica Russo, real backyard agronomists, who answered my call for help. Thank you to my husband, Tom, who does so much to support my writing. I am also indebted to Kellogg's for Brown Sugar Cinnamon Pop-Tarts.

Thanks to my prayer partners on this book, Tessie Russo, Anne Russo Penaz, Missy Tippens and Mary Curry.

I always thank my agent, Meredith Bernstein, and my editor, Giselle Regus, because I know how blessed I am to have them on my team.

Chapter One

Maggie Jones lifted her head from the pages of the technical manual. Fire-alarm horns blared in the distance.

Six long blasts and one short.

Though technology had come to Paradise, Colorado, the old fire horns were still on duty. When Maggie was young and spent all her summers in Paradise, she could pinpoint the location of fires by counting the blasts. Back only a week, she was out of practice.

Through the repair store's big glass window she noted the clear, baby-blue sky painted with wisps of clouds. At a little past 1:00 p.m. on a Wednesday, it was cool for June, barely seventy degrees. A breeze blew in through the screened front entrance and slid over Maggie before moving out through the rear of the shop.

Maggie sniffed the air and sure enough she

did smell smoke. It was awfully close, and had a pungent odor. Almost like…eggs.

Eggs?

The manual flew through the air as she whipped open the door that divided the store and ran into the back room.

Black smoke billowed from a small kettle on a hot plate. With the current wind direction, most of the smoke was being sucked outside through the screen door, right into the alley.

"No. No. No."

Two hours ago she'd set the eggs to boil.

Two hours since she'd been lost reading about the intricacies of a computerized toaster. Who'd have thought three little eggs could produce so much foul-smelling smoke?

"I am doomed." As she mumbled the words, the door behind her flew open and bounced on its hinges, then slammed against the wall.

He filled the doorway.

A fireman clad in a heavy, mustard-and-gray jacket, carrying a red ax. His features were obscured by a yellow helmet and face mask. Intense eyes assessed her and the situation.

Although he was a large man, he moved quickly. In two strides he'd crossed the room and reached in front of her to tug the hot-plate cord from the wall. With a gloved hand he grabbed the handle of the blackened aluminum pot and tossed it into the sink.

Before Maggie could blink, he aimed the shop's fire extinguisher and blasted away. The little kettle rattled against the porcelain sink. Yanking off his gloves, he propped open the back door to further ventilate the room.

"Code 10-35. Under control. Over." His words, spoken into the field radio, were clipped as he nodded toward the front of the store, indicating Maggie should follow. She did, reading the back of his heavy coat. *Chief MacLaughlin, PVFD.*

In the front room two more firefighters guarded the store. Chief MacLaughlin waved them outside with the mere flick of his wrist and forefinger.

Outside on the front walk, yet another set of firemen stood shoulder-to-shoulder in front of Paradise's Engine Number One, where the vehicle's red and blue lights were still flashing.

Maggie grimaced. All this because she craved an egg salad sandwich.

"Don't move." The chief's gaze pinned her. "I'll be back."

Pressing herself against the cool metal counter, Maggie obeyed, while whispering a silent plea for heavenly assistance under her breath.

He moved through the crowd gathering on the sidewalk to speak to his men, who shot curious glances through the window at her.

Maggie looked away and hung her head for a moment before attempting to rally. *Come on,*

Maggie. Pull it together. What would Uncle Bob do?

Her favorite uncle would laugh and say this was good for business and probably announce a fire sale. If only Maggie was that confident. A mere twenty-four hours ago she'd sent Uncle Bob on a three-week fishing trip with assurances that she would run the fix-it shop and take care of everything.

She'd taken care of things, all right. Nearly burned down his livelihood.

Though she tried not to, she heard her parents and ex-fiancé whispering accusations in her ear. *Maggie Jones has done it again. Gotten lost in her little world, forgetting everything going on around her.*

They were right. Only this time she would have to deal with Captain Macho for her sins. Maggie grasped her ponytail and pulled it tight. She slid her glasses to the top of her head and rubbed the bridge of her nose.

She began to count to ten. She'd give her Aunt Betty that long to show up. As for her cousin Susan, she could probably stop at five.

"Mags. Nice job."

"Five," Maggie said aloud as Susan pushed her way through the sidewalk gawkers and firemen groupies and into the store.

Susan smiled, smoothed her blond coif and adjusted her silk sheath. "I'm so impressed. It seems I have underestimated you, cousin. Leave it to you to think of smoke to attract Jake."

Maggie frowned. "Who is Jake?"

"That would be me."

Both women turned.

"Excuse us, Susan," Chief Jake MacLaughlin said as he tugged off his helmet. "I'd like to have a word with your cousin."

Susan slipped out, and a familiar gray head peeked in; Aunt Betty, wearing a flour-dusted canvas apron over her slacks and a blouse.

"Margaret. Oh, my dear. Are you all right? I was helping out at Patti Jo's Café and Bakery when I heard the sirens."

"Everything is fine, Mrs. Jones. False alarm. I'll be through with your niece in a minute. Just a little paperwork. Would you please wait outside?"

"Yes, Chief," her aunt said, immediately backing up.

Maggie looked Jake MacLaughlin up and down.

"You do that quite well," she stated.

"Do what?" He narrowed his eyes.

"Take charge. You silenced both Susan and my aunt."

"Practice." He shrugged, pulled out a pen and began to write on an official-looking, aluminum clipboard.

Practice? Or perhaps it was the uniform that

added to the aura of power and strength. His well-worn gray-and-mustard coat covered wide shoulders and fell open in front to reveal red suspenders over a navy T-shirt.

Maggie assessed him with the due diligence granted any new problem. With pragmatic order she took in each detail, from his boots—size thirteen—to his face. She estimated his age somewhere around forty.

His skin was lightly tanned, an almost golden shade. Laugh lines accented the corners of his eyes. Dark stubble shadowed his cheekbones and chin. He hadn't shaved today. Maybe it was his day off?

She knew that Paradise's fire department consisted of a volunteer crew. *So what else did the man do?*

Curious, she continued to stare.

Chief MacLaughlin rubbed a hand over his forehead, pushing short, sun-streaked brown hair up and away from his damp skin. Turning slightly, his gaze locked with hers. His irises were amber with dark rims. Dark lashes framed his eyes. The entire effect reminded her of a lion.

Noting her inspection, his eyes widened. He blinked and cleared his throat.

"So you're Susan's cousin?"

"Yes. I'm Maggie Jones."

"You're nothing like Susan."

She winced. The man had a knack for the

obvious. No, she was nothing like Susan. Maggie was the geeky tomboy, and Susan, the beautiful former beauty queen.

Why was it that this time, in front of this particular man, the truth pinched like a pair of too-small shoes, constantly reminding a person they didn't fit?

Maggie found herself suddenly conscious of her shapeless gray T-shirt, ancient jeans and well-worn, black high-tops. She clamped her arms tightly across her chest and resisted the urge to hide her glasses in her pocket.

"I didn't mean—" he said.

"Oh, I get it," she interrupted, with a dismissive wave of her hand.

His lips formed a tight line, as Jake frowned. "No, ma'am. I don't think you do."

A knock on the glass outside the window caught her attention. A young fireman grinned at them, and then offered a thumbs-up gesture with a questioning expression.

Jake returned the thumbs-up and turned back to Maggie. "Look, it's the middle of the week and I've got four men outside who left their regular jobs to be here. I'll have to leave explanations for another time."

A palpable silence stretched between them as he flipped open the metal notebook.

"Identification?"

"Identification? But I told you. I'm Maggie

Jones. You know my aunt, Betty Jones. This is Uncle Bob's shop."

He nodded. "Still need your ID."

"Sheriff Lawson can vouch for me."

"Sam and his deputy are on a call. Normally they'd be here taking a report, as well."

Maggie reached over the counter for her purse. She released a short breath and handed him her driver's license.

He took the laminated card and placed it on top of the paperwork. "Denver? What brings you to our town?"

"I've been coming to Paradise for years. Why, I spent every summer here with my aunt and uncle when I was a kid. I'm practically a native."

"For years?" His gaze met hers. "How is it I've never met you?"

"You're older than me."

"Ouch." This time *he* winced.

"I didn't mean… I just meant…" She closed her mouth before her other foot attempted to jump in, as well.

"You know, I think I vaguely remember you," he returned. "Skinny kid with big glasses and braids. You followed Susan around."

"Touché," Maggie muttered. "And as you can see, I haven't changed all that much."

He raised a brow. "A little sensitive?"

"Not at all."

"If you say so." His face gave away nothing. "Denver is your current address?"

"No. I'm, well, sort of in flux." Maggie pulled on a hangnail. "Right now, I'm staying on Mulberry Lane."

"Susan's old place?"

She nodded as her distracted gaze took in his large hands. Capable hands.

"Phone number?"

"Phone number?" she repeated, confused.

He tapped the clipboard. "For the paperwork."

Maggie rattled off her cell-phone number. "You aren't going to charge me for this little visit, are you?"

"The fire department is a service of the town. Can't remember charging anyone before." His gaze met hers. "Unless you plan to be a repeat offender."

Her head jerked up. "Of course not."

His lips twitched. "How long will you be in town?"

"That's a little hard to say. At least three weeks. I'm managing the shop while my Uncle Bob is fishing."

"Fly-fishing. Best time of year. Spring runoff. We're really going to be slammed with tourists when tournament registration begins."

"Tournament?"

"Fishing tournament on the Rio Grande."

"I imagine that's good for the economy," she said.

"It is." He nodded. "Then back to Denver?"

"What?" She cocked her head.

"Then you'll be heading back to Denver?"

"Is this for your report, as well?"

"Just being neighborly, ma'am."

Ma'am? The cockles of her heart were officially rankled. "I don't know what I'll be doing in three weeks, Chief MacLaughlin. Praying about what I want to be when I grow up, I imagine."

He blinked and froze. Then he began to laugh, a deep, rich sound that took Maggie by surprise. His eyes did crinkle at the corners as she suspected they would, making his face open up with even more masculine appeal.

Charming. That was the first word that popped into her head. Yes. He was charming. Far too charming for her own good.

"I was being serious," she finally said. More serious than he would ever understand.

"I'll bet you were." Chief MacLaughlin grabbed his helmet and gave her a short salute. "Pleasure to meet you, Maggie Jones. Stay safe."

"Ah, um, yes. Thank you," Maggie said, her face heating at the sound of her name on his lips.

Her gaze followed him out to the street, where he climbed into the passenger side of the truck, his movements lithe and easy, despite the heavy layers of gear.

The fire engine's horn sounded before the vehicle pulled away from the curb.

Maggie shook her head, willing herself out of the daze that had wrapped itself around her.

"I'm simply going to have to stay out of his way," she murmured. "Because Jake MacLaughlin is an exceptionally dangerous man."

"Attention, shoppers. We're serving free coffee and carrot-cake muffins with lemon icing from Patti Jo's Café and Bakery at the front of the store."

Jake looked up from the paperwork on his desk as the announcement blared over the hardware-store loudspeaker.

What's he up to now? Ever since he'd semiretired, Jake's father spent his extra time divided between his newly self-appointed roles as marketing director for the store and head of Jake's nonexistent reelection committee. Jacob "Mack" MacLaughlin Senior was oblivious to the fact that Paradise Hardware was the only hardware store in Paradise. There was no competition.

Jake set aside the monthly inventory folder and shoved back his chair. Taking long strides through the aisles he followed the scent of fresh coffee.

"Nice picture, Jake."

"Huh?" Jake turned.

At the end of aisle one, near the cash register, several customers were gathered around the *Paradise Gazette* as they munched their muffins.

One of the regulars shoved the front page of the paper at Jake. Smack-dab in the middle was a photo of him in turnout gear standing next to Maggie Jones.

She looked like she'd taken a bite out of something sour.

Great. Just great. It had been pretty obvious yesterday that she wasn't in awe of the truck or the uniform like most of the women in town. He could almost feel her glare from the two blocks that separated the hardware store and the fix-it shop. Somehow the photo op would turn out to be his fault, adding fuel to her ire. The woman didn't like him. Of that, Jake was certain. Why that bothered him, he didn't know, but it did.

His father clapped him on the back. "Nice picture, huh?"

"Dad, how did they get this picture?"

Ever happy-go-lucky, Mack grinned and ran a hand through his thick, silver hair. "Me. I took it through the window of Bob's shop. Told you that photography class would come in handy. Great publicity, huh? The election is coming up, after all."

"I'm running unopposed."

"No matter. This will hit home with the voters. You're a hero, Jacob."

"Burned eggs, Dad. It was a 10-35. Unnecessary alarm system activation."

"Who's that in the picture with you?" Mack asked.

"Maggie Jones. You'll note that she doesn't look real happy."

Mack narrowed his eyes and pulled the paper close to his bifocals. "Can't hardly see her face. Bob's niece, right?"

"Yeah."

"She's a smart one, that girl. I brought that broken reel of mine to her and she figured out what was wrong with it before I even left the shop. You know, the one you've been working on?"

Jake gave a tight nod.

"I heard from Duffy that you two really hit it off."

"Duffy said that?"

"Said it sure took you a long time to get her statement."

Jake folded up the newspaper. "Don't listen to Duffy, Dad. He's a troublemaker."

"He's your best friend."

"Not anymore." Jake handed his father the paper.

Mack laughed and shot a glance at the big, stainless-steel wall clock. "Hey, I nearly forgot.

Bitsy Harmony called. She said to remind you that you've got an appointment at the photographer's."

"Tell me again why I'm going to the photographers?"

"The fire department fund-raiser at the Paradise Fair."

"The raffle." Jake bit out the words.

"Right."

"Bitsy says it's going to bring in lots of revenue for the fire department as well as the auxiliary. A win-win for everyone."

"Since when did you get so tight with Bitsy?"

"We're friends. Nothing wrong with that, is there?"

Jake grunted in response, as his mood moved south. Bitsy's first idea had been a bachelor auction. He'd thought he'd effectively torched that notion, but when he hadn't been looking the raffle had taken off like a bottle rocket.

He had to give the woman credit. This time the head of the Paradise Ladies Auxiliary had played it smart. She'd gotten a fire started on the raffle before he'd had a chance to snuff it out. The entire town, including Jake's own men, had embraced the idea. All he could do now was smile and go along with it.

Because, yeah, it *was* an election year.

"Think you could watch the store while I go?" Jake asked.

"Sure. Glad to help you out. But come right

back. I've got a meeting with our web guy at noon. He drove all the way up here from the Springs."

"We have a web guy? I thought Duffy was doing the webpage."

"Bitsy says it's time for us to go pro, son."

Bitsy again?

His father continued. "This guy is going to redesign the site and get the store some social media. Good for business. Might even get us Tweeter next."

"Twitter."

Mack released a hearty chuckle. "Is that what it's called?"

Jake shook his head as he exited and walked across the blacktop to his truck.

He started the engine and pulled out of the parking lot, making a hard right at the last minute. Why not take the long way around to the photography studio, past Bob Jones's shop? Make sure everything was okay with his fellow shopkeepers.

Or possibly, just one Maggie Jones.

He'd never admit it to anyone, but he'd been thinking about her a lot since yesterday. Maybe it was her jaunty ponytail the color of warm caramel. Or the way she chewed on her lower lip as she concentrated. Or the way she looked at him, with those owlish brown eyes that seemed to see...*everything*. Next to her cousin Susan, a man might overlook the mousy brunette.

That would be a mistake.

It was the strangest thing, he mused. The incident report paperwork should have taken five minutes, tops. But he couldn't stop asking questions. Couldn't say what had gotten into him, either. Except that Maggie Jones disturbed him. That concerned Jake, because he hadn't been disturbed in a very long time.

At his age he had no energy to put into women. Generally he didn't have to, either. Since his wife died, women naturally seemed to think he needed taking care of. He didn't. Unfortunately, that didn't stop them from trying to get his attention, though he'd never shown an interest before.

Thankfully things were slowing down. Of the twenty-two men on the Paradise Volunteer Fire Department, he was one of the oldest. Lately he'd started to feel his age.

Jake inhaled as he glanced out the window of his pickup toward the outline of the Sangre de Cristo Mountains in the distance. The scent of pine and clean air, mixed with all that was Paradise, filled his senses.

Paradise had healed Jake more than he deserved. More than he could have ever hoped. He could never finish paying penance for his sins. For the life lost that day ten years ago. He knew it and he assumed God knew, as well. Still he managed to get through each day with a smile and a sense of humor. That was all a man could ask. Right?

Or maybe not. All he knew for sure was that in the last twenty-four hours he'd started thinking about things he never imagined he'd have a chance to ever consider again.

The wind shifted and Jake smelled something else in the breeze. Change. Yeah. He knew it was coming, yet he didn't embrace the fact. No, these days he was only wary. Maybe a little scared, too.

"What lies ahead, Lord?" Jake murmured. "Prepare me. Whatever it is."

Chapter Two

Maggie reached for her denim jacket and headed outside, where Susan waited at the curb in a gleaming, red convertible sports car. Her husband, Al, owned a new-car dealership in Monte Vista and humored his wife by letting her test-drive a vehicle every now and again. Maggie pulled open the door and slid in.

She looked over at Susan, who wore a bright red halter sundress, the exact shade of her car, and a wide-brimmed straw hat. Then she glanced down at her own jeans and beige scoop-neck top. "I'm underdressed." The words were a dour admission.

"No worries." Susan smiled. "We'll get you into my boutique this week and liven up your wardrobe."

Maggie mustered a weak smile.

"Any problems with the house?" Susan asked.

"No. It's perfect. I've already planted herbs.

I've got a spot along the fence where I'm going to set up my hives, and next week I'll start planning my garden."

"Wait a minute. Back up. Hives? As in bees?"

"Yes. I've ordered two honey-bee boxes."

"Bees. Okay." Susan shook her head. "Bees aside, how is the house itself? There's not much furniture in there."

"Enough for me. Right now, I'm just grateful it was available."

"Truly a God thing," Susan said. "We nearly sold the place, but the deal fell through at the last minute."

"I'm very grateful to you and Al for letting me rent it from you."

"I don't want your money. You're family."

"I need to pay my way, Susan."

"Fine for now, Mags, I'm just thrilled to have you back in Paradise," Susan said.

Maggie shook her head. "I didn't realize how much I missed you and your folks and Paradise until this week."

"Well, it's awfully sweet of you to give Daddy the chance to go fishing. This is his best birthday present ever. Not many people would dare to take on a shop that fixes everything from bicycles to computers."

"Eclectic. Not unlike me. It makes perfect sense for me to run the shop, and I really enjoy it."

She did, and she loved taking things apart and

repairing them. In a perfect world she'd hang out at the shop on a regular basis. Unfortunately her bank account didn't agree. A real job was her next priority.

She wasn't going to think about the one she'd quit in Denver, nor her recent and depressing past. Not today. Today was Saturday and another day toward the future. A future she would choose. Not her parents.

They drove down the main drag of Paradise, toward the outskirts of town, where the ballpark and the new fairgrounds waited.

"Where am I volunteering?" Maggie asked, taking in the view of the tall conifers that lined the road.

"The bait shop."

Maggie shot straight up in her seat. "The bait shop? Of all the places to volunteer, you pick the bait shop? I don't know anything about fishing."

"Think, Maggie. Where will all the men be? Where they sign up for their fishing license, of course."

"Yes. Of course. No-brainer." Maggie nodded. "What I don't understand is why you think I care? I only just recently got rid of a man. I am not looking for another."

"Margaret Jones, are you going to sit there and tell me you didn't find Jake MacLaughlin to be the best-looking man you have ever set your eyes upon."

"What does *he* have to do with this conversation?" Maggie sputtered.

"Answer my question."

"Oh, he's handsome, all right, if that's what you're asking."

"I thought so." Susan released a satisfied smile.

"You're married. Why are you looking?"

"I'm merely prescreening the field as my duty to you."

Maggie released an unladylike snort.

"You never know," Susan continued, "Jake could be your one."

"*One* what?"

"The one."

"Susan, I already met the one, and as it turned out he was only interested in me because of the potential for a tenure recommendation from my parents."

"That man was *one loser.* You were smart to run."

"Tell that to my parents, who are no doubt, right this moment, returning several dozen wedding presents."

Susan shrugged. "So the timing wasn't the best."

An understatement. Maggie sighed, recalling the hefty check she'd sent her parents to cover the cost of the last-minute wedding cancellations.

"Let's focus on the positive." Susan reached over and patted Maggie on the arm. "Lucky for you, Al and Daddy won't be back for another nineteen days. I can devote all my extra time to helping you."

Maggie slouched down against the hand-stitched, leather bucket seats. "Save me, Lord," she mumbled as Susan zipped the little red car into the fairgrounds parking lot.

The bright banner across the front entrance proclaimed Paradise's annual Fair. In smaller print attendees were reminded that all proceeds supported the Paradise Volunteer Fire Department and the Paradise Ladies Auxiliary. Susan quickly located a spot dismissed as too small in the sea of monster pickup trucks and pulled in.

Maggie got out of the car and stretched while she waited for Susan to remove her stuff from the trunk. Barely holding back a huge grin she glanced around at all the families headed toward the fairgrounds. Tipping her head back she let the warm sun kiss her face. It didn't get any better than this—small town, population seventeen hundred and four, unobstructed view of the San Juan Mountains to the west, the Sangre de Cristo Mountains to the east and brilliant powder-blue skies as far as she could see.

A thud from the trunk interrupted her musings. Maggie turned. "Susan, do you need help?"

"No, no, I'm just doing a quick check. One of my girls is manning a booth for the boutique. I brought along some extra inventory." She popped her head up from the car's trunk and waved a hand. "Go ahead. I don't want to make you late… The bait-shop tent is right next to the information booth. I'll come and get you for the big raffle. Remember, it's in about two hours."

Maggie set off, a silly grin on her face as she took in the sights. The smell of waffle cakes, sausages and barbecued turkey legs teased her senses. Barely eleven in the morning, and already lines were forming.

She dodged a teenage couple with arms looped around each other, and then stopped midstep at a huge poster tacked to the side of the information booth.

Jake MacLaughlin, his strong profile set against a background of muted red, white and blue. The sign read Reelect the Chief.

The man was everywhere. She hurried her steps, navigating around people to get to the large bait-shop tent set up by the chamber of commerce. There was a crowd gathered outside, waiting to get licenses. Fishing was one of the biggest tourist draws to Paradise in the summer months.

Maggie grabbed a carpenter's apron and an instruction sheet from the cashier and got to work. It took less than thirty minutes for Maggie to get through the first deluge of customers. She turned her attention to stocking a table with applications for fishing licenses and entry forms for the upcoming midsummer fishing tournament on Paradise Lake.

Suddenly goose bumps danced over her arms. She looked up. Jake MacLaughlin had walked into the tent. Maggie slipped her glasses into her pocket and adjusted her ponytail. When Jake's glance met hers she knew exactly what he was thinking.

Trouble.

She read the words on his face. The man thought she was trouble. He turned slightly as though to leave, then he suddenly did an about-face, and walked over.

"Don't say it," she said.

"Say what?" he asked. His jungle-cat eyes twinkled and it was clear he had failed at all attempts to keep a straight face.

"'Burned any eggs, lately?'"

"You got it all wrong. I was going to ask if you'd seen your picture in the newspaper," he said.

"Could we not talk about that, either?"

"Fine by me."

She willed herself to concentrate on dividing up the supply of pens.

Jake cleared his throat. "Mind if I fill out an application?"

Maggie's face warmed. "Sorry. Fishing license or tournament application?"

"Both."

Of course he was an overachiever. She handed him the forms and tried not to stare as he filled them out. Maggie was used to tall, wiry academics with pale skin. Jake MacLaughlin was larger than life, with the build of a football player. Yet, he seemed keenly intelligent. A puzzle. She liked puzzles.

He lifted his head and met her gaze.

"What?" he asked.

"Nothing." She glanced away, her face heated yet again.

When she turned back he held out two twenty-dollar bills.

"May I see some ID?" she asked.

"You're kidding, right?

She shrugged. "No ID, no entry."

"Turnabout, huh?"

"I don't know what you mean."

"Right." He flipped out his billfold and Maggie took her time reading the birth date on the license. It was exactly as she suspected. Midlife crisis waiting to happen.

"Here you go," she said. "Your entry ticket, plus a coupon for a free cupcake from Patti Jo's Café and Bakery."

"You keep the coupon." He patted his stomach. "I'm watching my calories."

Her gaze was drawn to his flat abdomen, broad muscular chest and biceps. Oh, he looked good in the navy T-shirt with the fire-company logo on it, the cotton fabric stretched taut against his muscles. And he knew it. She barely managed to maintain her "I am not impressed" stance.

They both turned as a crowd of people entered the tent. When the group moved toward the registration table, Jake was effectively trapped behind the table with Maggie.

"Hey, Chief. Working hard?" A young man with a navy shirt that matched Jake's smiled and winked at Maggie.

"You know it," Jake returned.

To Maggie's surprise he didn't leave her side but began to hand out forms and pens.

"You don't have to stay," Maggie murmured.

"Are you trying to get rid of me?" Jake asked with a wry grin.

"No. I'm simply saying that I'm sure you probably have other places you need to be."

"Nope."

As the license lines grew, they developed a companionable and efficient pattern. Maggie collected the money, slipping it into her apron pockets, and Jake took the completed forms. She noted he didn't check ID as she had. Apparently he knew everyone in Paradise.

She remained acutely aware of his presence, especially the occasional moments their hands collided.

"Sorry," she said, drawing back quickly.

He mumbled an apology in return.

"Do you need to be somewhere?" she asked when there was a momentary lull.

"Trying to get rid of me yet again, huh? You know, a guy could get a complex around you."

"I'm *trying* to be polite. I appreciate your help. I don't think I could have handled that crowd alone."

Jake smiled. "Anytime."

"Anytime, what?" Susan interrupted as she walked into the tent.

"Anytime is a good time for fishing." Jake grinned. "Right, Maggie?"

"Yes. Correct." The brochures in her hand slipped to the table and she carefully collected them.

"Well, ladies," Jake said, "I guess I'll be off." He gave Maggie a quick wink.

Embarrassed, she only nodded, while Susan scrutinized them both.

"We should go," Susan said. "They're closing the tents for an hour during the raffle. I've already gotten us seats up close and personal."

Maggie took off her apron, turned her money in to the cashier and followed an impatient Susan.

"Hurry, hurry," her cousin urged, linking her arm through Maggie's. "We don't want to miss a thing."

"Isn't your mom here today?" Maggie asked, looking around.

"She's backstage helping the Paradise Ladies Auxiliary with the pies."

"Pies? Some sort of blue-ribbon thing?"

"Sort of. They raffle pies and cakes that were awarded ribbons earlier this morning. Then they'll start raffling all sorts of other delectable things."

Maggie followed Susan to a reserved seating area close to the stage. "How did you get these great seats?"

"Al is a sponsor."

"You know, I don't remember any fairs when I was growing up."

"That's because this is the first year." Susan handed Maggie five tickets. "For the dessert raffle. I put yours in for the chocolate éclairs. We want this to be a memorable day for you. Oh, and keep an eye on Bitsy Harmony's peach pie. Third from the left. I'm not letting anyone else beat me to that pie."

"Who is Bitsy Harmony?"

"Oh, you remember her. She's a close friend of my mother's. Tall with a silver-white bun on the top of her head? Bitsy runs the auxiliary and she's just the best pie baker in the valley."

"The name doesn't ring a bell."

"That's probably a good thing. It's best to stay under Bitsy's radar if you can."

"Duly noted."

Susan shoved a fistful of tickets into her purse.

"How many tickets did you buy for the peach pie?" Maggie asked.

"A few." Susan's laughter trilled into the air.

A moment later, the mayor picked up the microphone and, after a few ear-piercing squeals, began the event. It was a simple, organized process. Names were drawn from glass bowls that sat in front of each baked item.

After seeing all those tickets in her purse, it was no surprise when Susan's name was drawn for a peach pie. Her cousin claimed her prize with loud gushing noises of total and complete amazement. As she thanked the mayor, Susan made a brazen plug for her boutique.

One by one, the desserts began to disappear. Maggie was more than thrilled not to win one of the éclairs. There was absolutely no way was she going up on stage in front of the entire town.

When the stage was cleared, poster boards were set on display stands. Each had the handsome, smiling face of one of Paradise's single and therefore apparently, very eligible volunteer firefighters. If the excited thrum of female chatter was any indicator, this was going to be the highlight of the raffles.

Maggie glanced at each poster, noting Jake MacLaughlin's face on the last board. He took a good picture, she'd give him that. The photographer managed to catch that wounded-hero look in the black-and-white shot of him with his helmet on, the chin strap loose. The piercing cat eyes seemed to follow Maggie. And then there was that barely there smile on his full lips. It was almost as though he held a secret deep inside.

She pondered the thought for a moment, and then shook her head. What an imagination she had. Jake was hardly wounded. He seemed to be a carefree bachelor. No doubt there was a long trail of broken hearts behind him.

She turned and scanned the crowd, spotting him at the back, taking what looked to be a good-natured ribbing from his buddies. When his gaze connected with hers he shrugged his shoulders and grinned, unabashed.

"Unbelievable. Church ladies auctioning off men," Maggie said to Susan.

"No, no. Jake shot down the auction idea."

"Jake did?"

"Uh-huh. This is a raffle. No auctioning. If you win, for your ticket you get a date to the Founder's Day supper next Saturday with the fireman whose helmet your ticket was picked from. We raise money for a great cause, too."

"Remind me what cause that is."

"The Paradise Volunteer Fire Department and the Ladies Auxiliary. The auxiliary supports all the local churches, missions and other charitable causes. So we're giving to the Kingdom of God, as well. He would be very pleased."

Maggie opened her mouth at the logic and then

gave up. Who was she to judge? Besides, she suspected the Lord would advise staying out of this particular discussion.

Hoots and whistles exploded through the crowd as winning names were gingerly plucked from the inverted yellow helmets. Each winner enthusiastically claimed their poster and an envelope with tickets inside.

As each moment passed the mayor inched closer to Jake's poster. The crowd began clapping in a rhythmic pattern, chanting the name of Paradise's fire chief.

"This is getting exciting," Susan chirped.

"You think so?" Maggie barely resisted rolling her eyes.

"You bet I do." Susan leaned over to her large leopard satchel sitting on the floor. "Oh my. Silly me. I almost forgot. I bought you a few tickets." She thrust a stack of tickets at Maggie.

"Tickets?" Maggie startled, nearly falling out of her seat in an effort to gather the chain of paper as the roll tumbled from her lap onto the ground. "Susan. A few is like two or three." She blinked, stunned as realization hit. "Wait. A. Minute. What exactly are these tickets for?"

"Why, for Jake, of course. There's only a hundred and forty-seven." She frowned. "I thought I brought more money, but I left my checkbook in my other purse."

Maggie choked. *"One hundred and forty-seven tickets for Jake? Are you nuts?"*

"There's nothing I wouldn't do for my cousin and the firemen of Paradise. You know, Al's on the board of the PVFD. He'd be so proud of me for this."

As Maggie folded the tickets into an orderly pile the clapping ceased. People looked around the tent in wide-eyed anticipation.

A cold chill passed over Maggie. Mouth dry, she looked up at the stage and then to Susan.

The microphone screeched and crackled. "Is Margaret Jones here?"

"Susan," she slowly whispered through terse lips.

"Hush, now. You'll embarrass us in front of the mayor. Go on up there," her cousin admonished.

Maggie stood, swallowed and took a shuddering breath. Amid the cheers and applause she marched stiffly to the stage, grateful they were seated so close.

The mayor put his hand on her arm and spoke into the microphone. "Ah, just a minute there, Margaret." He glanced around. "I'm sure our citizens would like to meet Bob and Betty's niece. Margaret is managing the fix-it shop while Bob is gone fishing, and of course you all saw her face on the front page of the Paradise paper this week."

A wave of chuckles spread across the audience.

Maggie attempted a smile, knowing the result was sickly at best. She moved from the stage, down the stairs and directly past Susan and the crowd, her eyes fixed forward. Without thinking she kept walking until she reached the sanctuary of the bait tent.

Stunned, one hand clutched the envelope against her hammering heart. Her other hand held the tangled ball of ticket stubs. Jake's poster slid from under her arm as she sagged against the nearest table.

"So, we have a date." Jake's cheerful voice reached her before he did.

Startled, Maggie straightened. She carefully gathered her pride around her, but didn't face him. "I imagine you're used to this sort of thing.

"Used to it? No way. Though I will admit I'm relieved one of the ladies from the retirement home didn't win."

She dared to finally turn and look at him. Oh, those laughing eyes.

"Out of curiosity, how many tickets do you have there?" he asked.

"One hundred and forty-seven."

His eyes rounded. "Whoa. I'm not sure if I should be flattered or terrified."

"Neither. Susan bought them."

He frowned. "You don't sound very enthusiastic."

"Don't I?" She shoved the envelope into her

back pocket, and slid the poster and tickets under the table.

Jake rubbed his chin. "I hope you're not planning to back down. It wouldn't look good for the chief to get stood up."

"Yes, and in an election year, too."

Jake paused. "How'd you know about that?"

"Lucky guess." Maggie picked up a bottle of water from the table. Lifting it to her lips, she drained the entire eight ounces and then aimed for the recycle bin. Her shot was impeccable, echoing through the tent.

Fortified, she met Jake's gaze again. "Rest assured, I wouldn't dream of standing you up, Chief MacLaughlin. I'm going to think of this as my civic duty."

Chapter Three

"Here's the problem, Susan. I don't do dresses." Maggie glanced around the boutique from the door's threshold and shivered.

Susan patted Maggie's hand before gently urging her farther into the shop. "I know, honey, but you're going to have to work with me. I consider it a personal challenge to my creative genius to find you the perfect ensemble for this appointment with destiny."

Maggie closed her eyes and then opened them slowly. She was pretty certain she'd fallen into a Colorado rabbit hole and would never find her way out.

"Dresses aside, your entire wardrobe is a cry for help. Why, you don't own anything, besides blue jeans, that isn't in the neutral family."

Maggie would concede that on that particular point, unfortunately her trendy cousin was spot-on.

Susan continued. "You probably are unaware that I am the personal shopper for Bernice Harris."

"Bernice who?"

"Bernice Harris, the reigning Bison Queen of Paradise Valley. She'll be on a float during the parade Saturday."

"Parade?" Maggie frowned. "What parade?"

"This weekend is huge in Paradise. The Founder's Day parade is Saturday morning before the supper. Why, this weekend heralds the onslaught of tourist season. So you can see why we have our work cut out for us."

"We do?"

"Oh, yes. It's already Monday. You'll need several new outfits, besides a dress."

Maggie uttered a noncommittal sound as she considered a dash for the door. What was the point? Since they were kids Susan and her long legs had always arrived everywhere first.

"Did I tell you that Bernice asked me to go on tour with her? Naturally I turned her down. I'm needed here. This boutique is my calling. I'm sort of a missionary to the fashionless." Susan offered a benevolent smile. "You, my dear cousin, shall be my coup de grâce. If I can make you look good I can make anyone look good."

Maggie flinched at the words, before glancing at her utilitarian leather watch. "I'm on my lunch break."

"Enough time to get started."

Susan reached out a hand and plucked Maggie's tan cotton shirt between her thumb and forefinger. "These clothes you wear. They do nothing for you." She released the fabric and rubbed her hands together.

"What exactly did you have in mind, Susan?"

Susan's finely shaped brows knit together in deep thought. "Well, first, I'd like to see Chief MacLaughlin brought to his knees."

"This is not about Jake MacLaughlin," Maggie sputtered.

"When men are in the equation it's always about them."

"No! My goal is simply to not embarrass myself. Couldn't you help me to blend in? Not stand out."

Susan shook her head and sighed. "Maggie. Maggie. Maggie. You're the smartest woman I know. Assistant professor of physical science at age thirty-two. Dr. Margaret Jones. Very impressive." She crossed her arms and tapped her toe. "Why is it, do you suppose, that you have set such a low bar for your personal life?"

Susan's words hit the target with impeccable precision. "Um…I…" The air whooshed from Maggie's lungs, deflating her outrage.

Okay, fine. Susan was right. Maggie had spent a lifetime making her parents' priorities her priorities, barely eking out a life of her own. Truth be told, she'd never even lived on her own until now. Pretty much everything in her life was a reflection of her parents' choices.

"Well?" Susan asked as she continued to tap an annoying beat on the tile floor.

Resistance was futile. Maggie took a deep breath. "Fine. Let's do this."

"That's the attitude. Nothing like a little martyrdom to spark a well-deserved change."

Maggie glared.

"You go right into that first dressing room." Susan wiggled her fingers toward the back of the shop. "I'll bring you some things to try on."

No sooner had Maggie stepped into the tiny dressing room than the louver doors burst open and Susan entered with a tall stack of clothing in her arms.

"You can't be serious," Maggie said.

"We're simply checking for sizing. If they fit, put them in one pile. Those that don't fit you can put in another pile."

"Fit. I'll give you fit," Maggie muttered as she quickly held up each garment, discarding most as too revealing, clingy or outrageous.

"How are you doing in there?"

"All done." Maggie came out holding two hangers. One with an eyelet-trimmed, peach peasant blouse and the other with a pair of forest-green capris.

Susan looked from the garments to Maggie. "They aren't neutral, I'll give you that."

"Good. Right?"

"It's a start. Now look what I found in today's shipment from Denver." Susan waved a coral dress on a pink satin hanger through the air.

The fabric shimmered and shined in a manner that definitely said "look at me."

"A dress?" Maggie asked.

"Not just any dress, this is your dress for the supper. No point in trying anything else on. This is you, and there isn't another one like it in the area. You will be the envy of every woman in a twenty-five-mile radius." Susan shoved the dress at her. "I'll wait right out here."

Maggie slipped the confection over her head. "I can't breathe," she muttered, easing the fabric over her waist and setting it on her hips.

"Breathe later. Come on out here." Susan tugged on Maggie's arm, pulling her to the center of the shop.

"Oh, yes. Definitely, yes," Susan murmured.

"*Yes* what?"

"It's perfect."

Maggie smoothed down the bodice, appreciative of the modest neckline. The fabric nipped her waist then flared. A layer of sheer material covered the skirt as well as the cap sleeves, adding to the gossamer illusion.

Could she, Maggie Jones, pull off wearing a dress like this?

"Now wait right here, I'll pin the hem and—" Susan stopped midsentence. "I nearly forgot. I need to call and make a hair appointment for you at the Emporium before they're booked solid."

"There's nothing wrong with my hair."

Susan simply shook her head and walked away.

"I said, there's nothing wrong with my hair," Maggie called after her cousin. She pushed several loose strands back into her ponytail. Wandering around the shop, she stopped to examine a colorful array of silk blouses lined up on hangers like ice-cream parlor flavors in rainbow shades of raspberry, pistachio, lemon and peach.

Turning, Maggie caught her reflection in the mirror. At least she thought it was her. Hmm, it was like her head was on someone else's body. There was something special about the dress. Susan was right.

"Whoa."

"Excuse me?" Maggie whirled around, bumping into a display of scarves. Lace and satin slithered to the floor. Her gaze moved from the puddle of color on the floor to Jake MacLaughlin, who stared at her, his mouth agape.

He reached down to scoop up the material at the same moment she did. Their heads knocked.

"Sorry. You okay?" he asked.

"Yes." She rubbed her forehead. "Are you supposed to be in here?"

"Why wouldn't I?"

"Isn't it bad luck or something?"

"I think that's brides," Jake said, handing her back the pile of scarves.

"Oh." Maggie shoved the tangled material onto the glass display counter. "Did you need Susan?"

"Nope." He eyed her for a moment longer.

"Are you just going to stand there and stare at me?" she asked, her voice rising an octave.

His mouth curled into a slow grin. "I'm trying to decide."

"Stop that," she demanded, flustered.

"Stop what?"

"That smile."

"What's not to smile about? That's a nice dress."

"Right." Maggie inhaled. "Look, you're a very handsome man, and I am sure you are accustomed to women drooling over you—"

"Drooling?" He choked on a laugh.

"Yes."

"Wait, back up there a minute. You think I'm handsome?'

"Don't mess with me, Chief MacLaughlin." She headed toward the dressing room.

"Jake, it's Jake," he called after her. "And trust me, I am not messing with you."

Maggie stopped and glanced over her shoulder. "I guess you haven't noticed that half the women in this town are in love with you."

"Big on sweeping generalities, aren't you?"

"I'm not blind." She opened the louver door. "Stay right there."

Jake cleared his throat. "What is it about you? We always seem to get off on the wrong foot. You notice that?"

Maggie closed and locked the door before she quickly pulled off the dress, and tugged her jeans and shirt back on.

"Hello?" Jake called.

"I heard you." She marched out of the dressing room, her sneakers dangling from her fingers.

He tucked his hands into the back pockets of his jeans and leaned back on the heels of his boots, watching her. "I'm here because I was across the street when I saw you go into your cousin's shop. I need your phone number."

She shoved her feet into her sneakers and glanced across the street to the neatly painted gray building with gleaming windows. The perimeter of the property was surrounded by trimmed bushes and several black benches. A black awning announced it was a hardware store.

Maggie eyed Jake with renewed interest. "Nice store," she said as she leaned over to tie the laces on her high-tops.

"It is."

"I don't remember that building being there when I was a kid."

"Brand-new. Opened up about five years ago."

Silence stretched as Maggie again stared across the street.

"Your number?"

"Hmm?" She turned back to Jake. "I gave you my number the other day."

"That was for the report. I didn't actually save it. That would be a tad bit unethical." He handed her his cell.

"You need my number, why?"

"In case, oh, say I'm running late on Saturday due to a fire. Or I get lost."

Maggie narrowed her eyes and took the phone. She punched in her digits, casually, as though she gave men her number all the time.

"Well, well. Look who's here," Susan purred. "Can I interest you in anything, Chief MacLaughlin?"

"I'm good for now." He winked at Maggie as she handed him back his cell, then he did a neat about-face and headed out of the shop.

"What was that all about?" Susan asked.

"He needed my number for the…the Founder's Day thing."

Susan looked at his retreating form and then back to Maggie. "You have an appointment at eleven Thursday for your hair. I thought we could do lunch while we're out."

"Susan, I can't just leave the shop in the middle of the day. On a Thursday, no less. One of the busiest days of the week."

"Of course you can. Mother told me Beck Hollander is back from vacation. He'll cover for you."

"Beck who?"

"Didn't Daddy tell you? Beck works part-time a few days a week. He's going to be a senior this year. Kind of a strange nerdy kid, but real smart, too. He's been helping Daddy for a few years now."

"I'm sure Beck and I will get along just fine. I speak fluent nerd." Maggie's gaze drifted across the street to the hardware store. "Um, Susan, I have to run."

"What about the dress? It needs to be hemmed."

"Can we do that later? Maybe tonight?"

"Sure. I'm taking mom to Four Forks in about thirty minutes."

"Four Forks?"

"Little town, north of us. They have a yarn shop she likes to visit."

"Got it."

"I'll call you when we get back. We'll need to talk makeup and accessories, too."

"Makeup and accessories." She sighed, resigned. "Okay. Whatever."

Leaving the shop Maggie hurried crossed the street and pulled open the expansive glass doors of the hardware store. A heady excitement raced through her. She breathed deeply, and forced herself to relax. Now she was in her element. No need to rush the pleasure. Her steps slowed as she moved with purpose down the aisles, getting the lay of the land.

Birdseed and birdhouses. Nuts and bolts. Shiny tools. Pails and buckets. Even pots and pans. Oh, wow, there was even stick candy. Sassafras, horehound and peppermint.

Oh, this was a real, old-fashioned hardware store.

Her pulse quickened.

What clothing stores did for women like Susan, and bookstores did for her parents, well, *that* was what hardware stores did for Maggie. It was like coming home.

"Can I help you?"

Jake? Maggie's head jerked as she turned around. "What are you doing here?"

He glanced around curiously. "Why shouldn't I be here?"

Over an intercom a voice boomed. "Chief, you have a phone call."

"You work here?" She arched a brow.

"I own the place, Maggie."

A small gasp slipped from her lips. *"You own a hardware store?"* She barely squeaked out the words.

"Yeah, why?" He glanced back at her with

a confused frown. "Hang on a second, I'll be right back."

"He owns a hardware store," she murmured. How could she resist such a man? Handsome, charming, bigger than life and he owned a hardware store.

Certainly the Lord never promised life would be fair, but this was more than even she could handle at the moment.

She strode to the exit.

"Maggie, wait."

His words only increased her pace, as though a scary dog nipped at her heels.

"Maggie."

"I. Have. To. Go." Hands on the glass, she shoved open the door and ran, passing nearly a half a dozen small shops, until she was well around the corner and nearly to her uncle's place.

Dear Lord. Help me. I've only just gotten the pieces of my life glued back together.

She was naive and inexperienced and if she wasn't careful she'd give her heart away to a man who'd carelessly break it into little pieces…again.

"You're fast, I'll give you that," Jake said as he turned the corner a full minute after Maggie.

Thankfully she had stopped. Her brown eyes were wide as she stared at him. "Why didn't you tell me you own a hardware store?"

He rubbed his jaw as he considered the question. "Ah. You got me there."

Strands of silky brown hair had escaped her ponytail in places, the only indication that she had raced an entire block without breaking a sweat.

"What happened back there?" he asked.

She was silent, her eyes on the sidewalk.

Jake shook his head. "You know, maybe you and I should start over." He stuck out his hand. "Hi, I'm Jake MacLaughlin. Part-time volunteer fireman, full-time owner and manager of Paradise Hardware."

She raised her head and eyed his hand for a moment before finally placing her small one in his. It fit nicely.

Pink tinged her cheeks.

"And you are?" he nudged her along.

"Margaret Jones, assistant professor of physical science." She sighed. "Currently unemployed."

He nodded and reluctantly released her soft fingers. "Nice to meet you."

She gave him a short nod, and a grudging smile.

"A professor? Physical science? Really?"

"Yes." Her eyes brightened. "My area of specialty is agronomy."

"You don't look like an agronomist."

Maggie frowned, confusion in the depths of her dark eyes.

Jake couldn't resist a grin.

"You're kidding," she said flatly.

"I am."

"Do you know what agronomy is?" Maggie asked.

"No, but I have complete faith you're going to tell me when we have our date."

"It's not a date."

"Right. Right. Civic duty."

"I better go…" She turned.

"First-time customers get a ten-percent discount. There's a coupon on our new webpage."

Turning back toward him, her face lit up, and a smile curved her generous mouth.

Jake had a sudden notion that he'd like to keep Maggie Jones smiling all the time.

"Really?" she murmured.

"Yeah. We really have a webpage."

"I meant the coupon."

"That, too. We're having a big sale on fire extinguishers right now."

The smile slipped from her face. "Very funny."

"Sorry. I couldn't resist." Jake looked around. They were nearly to her shop and right around the corner from Patti Jo's Café and Bakery. "Why don't I buy you a cup of coffee?"

"No. But thank you. I really do have to get

back to the shop. There's a Beck Hollander coming by today."

"Beck? Good kid. A little strange, but a good kid."

"That's what Susan said."

"Have you decided if you're staying in Paradise yet?" Jake asked.

"Oh, that depends."

"On what?" he asked, once again prodding her for an answer.

"If I have a reason to stay."

He nodded and tucked her words away. "So I guess I'll see you on Saturday?"

"Yes. Saturday," she murmured.

Jake turned slightly and then paused and faced her again. "Are we—" he raised a palm "—okay?"

"Yes. It's all good," she said with a shaky laugh.

"You're sure? I have this unsettling feeling that I did something wrong. But I can't quite figure out what."

"No. It's me, not you."

He scratched his head. "I'll guess I'll have to take your word for it."

Jake stuck his hands in his pockets as he walked slowly back to the store, silently counting sidewalk cracks and pondering his conversation with Maggie. Was that a panic attack she'd had in the hardware store? Maybe she had medical issues? The woman was a mystery, that much was clear.

That didn't explain why his good intentions and resolutions disappeared when he was around her. It seemed the more he resisted, the closer he danced to the flame.

He stopped outside the Paradise Floral Shop and stared at a sign in the window.

Don't forget to order your date a corsage for the Founder's Day supper!

Despite what Maggie thought, it was a date. He'd call in an order later.

Right now he had to get back to the store.

He had just pulled open the glass door to the hardware store when the fire horns began to sound. Simultaneously his cell phone rang, the tune indicating a text.

Jake raced to the parking lot while reading the message.

10-24. Auto fire.

The address was Bob Jones's fix-it shop.

He swallowed hard and headed to the fire station while silently praying. Trouble seemed to court Maggie Jones.

Chapter Four

Maggie was wedged under the sink in the back room when the shop's front door opened. *Now what?* From the street the echoing rumble of the Paradise Volunteer Fire Department's pump engine could be heard as it finally departed.

She blew strands of hair out of her eyes and gave the pipe wrench a quick turn. Only early afternoon, yet she was more than ready to call it a day before anything else happened. The steely look Jake had given her as he assessed the smoldering remains of her uncle's ancient and battered Ford engine was enough to keep her praying for the Lord's protection and assistance to stay out of trouble and out of Jake's way, at least until the Founder's Day supper.

Apparently Jake was so fit to be tied he sent another fireman, Duffy McKenna, to fill out the report. Fine with her. Redheaded Duffy had a face full of freckles. He was sweet and he kept her laughing. Of course he wasn't as…well, as three-dimensional as Jake. In fact all the firemen were nice, and understanding. The only one glaring at her was the chief. It seemed that the word *accident* wasn't in his vocabulary.

"Hello?" a voice called out.

"Coming," Maggie returned.

She wiggled out from beneath the drain pipes and stood up, straightening her clothes as she approached the front counter. A dark-haired teenager stood straight and tall. His bright blue eyes, magnified behind black-framed glasses, darted around the room as he wiped his hands on his jeans. The kid seemed to be all arms and legs. An earbud was hidden beneath his black curls, and the other end of the cord dangled around his neck. A wrinkled, once-white T-shirt hung on his lank body. He adjusted his glasses and stared at a point beyond her right shoulder.

"Beck Hollander, I presume."

He nodded.

"Maggie Jones."

Silence.

"You help part-time in the shop."

Another nod.

"My uncle has gone fishing for a few weeks. Perhaps you'd prefer to wait until he returns."

"Why?"

"I don't want to be a bad influence. I am currently persona non grata with the PVFD."

Beck cleared his throat. "I heard."

"*Heard?* Heard what?" She grasped her ponytail and gave it a sharp pull, yanking the loose hair back into order.

"You burned a truck."

Maggie grimaced and wrapped her hands around the neck of the blender she had been working on prior to the fire drama earlier in the day. She concentrated on tightly winding the cord around the base.

"That's not exactly what happened, though I suppose the details don't matter, do they? Let's talk about you."

He said nothing.

Undeterred, Maggie pasted a smile on her face. "Senior?"

Short nod.

This was worse than the blind dates her parents had set her up with. If she'd learned anything from those disastrous experiences with scholarly types who were inflicted upon her with her parents' high hopes of a future academic progeny, it was that open-ended questions were the ticket.

"What are your plans after high school?"

"College."

She sighed, and continued, refusing to be defeated. "Major?"

"Engineering."

Ah. Gotcha, you little brainiac.

"Biomedical, civil, environmental, electrical, computer, mechanical, energy?"

"Electrical and computer engineering."

"Great. I double majored in agronomics and earth science at UC Davis. Recently finished my doctorate."

His jaw slackened. "You don't look like..."

"What? A smart girl?"

Beck's face turned solid red from his neck to the tips of his ears, which peeked out from his mop of hair. "I, uh...sorry."

Maggie laughed. "Please, I'm flattered. Most people don't think I look like a professor, either."

His Adam's apple bobbed. "You're a professor?"

"Was. Physical science. I'm currently between jobs. And to be clear, I'm an assistant professor."

"Why teaching, when you could..." He gestured with a wave of a skinny arm.

"Oh, you know. Sometimes it's easier to go along to get along. Ironically, as it turns out, I like teaching." Maggie lowered her voice. "But I'll tell you a secret, someday I'm going to open my own nursery. I'm thinking about my own line of honey. Organic lavender, too." She shrugged. "I don't know how or when, but someday."

A smile spread on the kid's narrow face.

Yes! The barrier had been breached.

"So, anything in particular I need to know about your hours, Beck?"

He shook his head.

"What do you do around here?" Maggie asked.

"I handle most of the computerized repairs. Before your uncle left I rewired the shop's security alarm system. Now it can be set remotely."

"Really?"

"Yeah. Bob, uh, Mr. Jones isn't into digital stuff."

"So, do you get a lot of computerized repairs in Paradise?"

"No, but we get a lot of people stopping by for computer help."

"Uncle Bob dispenses computer advice?"

"No. I do. Mr. Jones doesn't even have a computer."

Maggie laughed. "Now that sounds like Uncle Bob. So, do you charge for this advice?"

"No. It's free. I'm like a tutor."

"A tutor? I like that. Maybe we can share the workload."

Beck grinned. "Sure. Yeah."

"How many hours are you working in the summer?"

"Three or four hours a day. Four days a week. I'm taking a few online classes, as well."

"All right. Works for me. I'm closing up shop here shortly." She met his gaze. "I've got an appointment Thursday around eleven. Think you could come in then and cover for me for a few hours?"

"Sure."

"And we can talk some more, maybe work on your schedule?" she added.

His eyes lit up. "Yeah. That'd be sweet."

"Sweet it is." Maggie stuck out her hand. "So I'll see you tomorrow."

"Yeah." He shook her hand. "Thanks, Ms. Jones."

"Maggie. Just Maggie."

"Um, Maggie?"

"Yes?"

He adjusted his glasses with his thumb and forefinger. "Chief MacLaughlin was wrong."

"Excuse me?"

"The 2003 Ford F-150 was recalled for suspected engine fires caused by a cruise control switch."

Maggie's mouth opened as his words sank in. "What?"

"Apparently, the problem is that the brake fluid leaks through the cruise control's deactivation switch into the system's electrical components, leading to corrosion and producing a buildup of electrical current that causes overheating and, in your case, fire."

"You know this, how?"

He shrugged. "I read a lot.

"You read a lot," she murmured. Suddenly his words clicked. "So it's not my fault?"

"Nope."

This time she smiled.

"I, uh, just thought you should know."

Vindication!

Her elation was short-lived as she realized she was the designated adult in this conversation.

"Thank you, Beck. I appreciate that. More than you know." She took a deep breath. "However, let's not be too hard on the chief. He's doing his job, and keeping everyone in Paradise safe certainly can't be easy."

Beck nodded yet again, and then looked at his sneakers.

"Was there something else?" she asked.

"Yeah. There's an opening at the high school."

"An opening? For what?"

He barely met her gaze. "Science teacher. I heard my dad talking about it last night. Mrs. Janson is going on maternity leave early. I thought maybe you might be interested."

Maggie's heart soared. She swallowed. "Are you sure?"

"Yeah. My dad is the principal."

"Oh."

"I'll tell him to call you," he added with a small smile, before he loped out of the shop.

"Yes. Please. Do that." Maggie was still staring after him, minutes later.

A job in Paradise?

Why not? Her credentials were impeccable. Of course, she'd have to be extremely careful from now on. No more accidental fires. Low profile. That was the ticket.

Mustn't get your hopes up, Margaret. The voice of her mother—the eternal pessimist—whispered in Maggie's ear.

"You're wrong, Mom. This job is mine. The Lord brought me to Paradise and He's not going to leave me sitting outside the Promised Land."

Maggie smiled and lifted her hand in a high five.

"Thank You, Lord."

Jake gripped the keys to his pickup tightly in his hand as he stood on the bottom step of Maggie's house. Bright red ceramic pots were arranged on her small porch with small painted signs identifying the plants—lemon thyme, cinnamon basil, chocolate mint and pineapple sage. He shook his head. He'd never even heard of half the stuff she'd planted.

Overhead the sky rumbled a warning that a storm was imminent. Undeterred, Jake walked up the steps and pushed the doorbell.

The teal-blue door of the cottage swung open and Maggie stared at him from behind the screen.

"I have it on good authority that it wasn't my fault," she announced.

"Hi, to you, too, Maggie."

Her cheeks flushed and she crossed her arms.

Jake glanced past her into the sparsely decorated living room. "Nice house. I presume your smoke detectors are in place and the batteries are up-to-date."

"Presume away."

"Maggie."

"They're fine. I checked everything when I moved in."

"Thank you."

"To what do I owe the honor of this visit, Chief MacLaughlin? Or do you routinely make smoke-detector house calls?"

"I'm following up to make sure you're okay." He frowned. "And I thought we were on a first-name basis?"

"So this is an official visit from the chief of the Paradise Volunteer Fire Department regarding the incident at 1233 Central Avenue?" She began to shut the door. "I'm fine. Thank you."

"Maggie."

The door stopped moving. "I told you, it wasn't my fault."

"Is that right?"

"Yes. Beck said so."

"Beck said so?"

"Something about a manufacturer recall due to known fire-related problems."

"Great, but I'm not blaming you."

"No?"

"No. May I come in?"

She averted her gaze. "That doesn't seem like a wise move to me."

Jake paused, realization dawning. "Are you afraid of me, Maggie?"

She opened her mouth and closed it. Then the screen door opened and Maggie stepped out onto the small porch as though eager to prove him wrong.

"I know you're really here to read me the riot act and I'd rather you did it out here, if you don't mind."

He met her gaze head-on. She didn't even blink as he towered over her and her ponytail. The woman was gutsy. He'd give her that.

Jake dialed down his menacing facade. It wasn't working anyhow.

"This is serious, Maggie."

She rubbed her arms against a sudden breeze that kicked up, bringing with it the scent of the pine trees surrounding the house.

"What exactly is serious?" she asked.

"When you smelled smoke you should have gotten out of the vehicle and called 9-1-1."

"I did call 9-1-1."

"After you raised the hood."

Her eyes rounded. "Who told you?"

"Who didn't?"

Maggie shook her head in disgust. "It was only an electrical fire."

"One out of seven fires involves vehicles. One out of ten fire deaths results from vehicle fires," Jake said.

"You memorized those stats?"

"It's my job."

"Fair enough, but I'm telling you it was barely a fire. Barely. Tiny flame. Very tiny.

"And yet you needed a fire extinguisher."

"Well. Um, yes."

"Where'd you get the fire extinguisher?"

"Your father gave it to me."

"My father?"

"Tall man. Silver hair."

"I know who my father is. In fact his house is right down the street a couple of blocks."

"Well, your father dropped the extinguisher off after the, um, first, um, incident. Said it was a 'welcome to Paradise' gift, since I'd *extinguished* the other one. Apparently all the MacLaughlins have a dark sense of humor."

Jake ignored the comment and made a mental note to talk to his father about meddling in his life. Again. "So are we clear?" he asked. "Next time call 9-1-1 immediately and move away from the vehicle."

She gave a solemn nod. "I can assure you that there won't be a next time."

"Yeah. Let's hope you're right." He cleared

his throat, grasping for a reason to keep chatting, knowing he was being off-the-wall ridiculous. He had things to do at home. Right? Feed the dog. Throw in a load of laundry. Yet, here he stood.

"Sorry about your truck," he said. "It's a complete write-off. You'll need to call the insurance company."

"It's not mine. It's Uncle Bob's shop truck." Maggie sighed. "Fortunately, I have a perfectly good bicycle that my aunt and uncle have kept for me since my last visit."

"Your last visit? When was that?"

"I was thirteen."

"Thirteen?" He stared at her. "You don't own a vehicle?"

"I left my car in Denver. It belongs to my parents. So you can see that the chances of another engine fire are pretty much nil."

"How did you get to Paradise?" he asked.

"Cab."

"You're joking, right? A cab all the way from Denver? That's like three and a half hours."

She stood straight and balled her small hands into fists. "Look, for your information, I was in a bit of rush when I left and there aren't any buses to Paradise."

"Whoa there. No need to get all excited."

Maggie released a breath and continued to stare him down.

"Are you in some kind of trouble?" he murmured.

Her cheeks flushed. She chewed on a ragged thumbnail and glanced around. "No. Of course not."

"You're sure? You can tell me, you know."

Maggie began to laugh. "What are you saying? You won't think any less of me if I confide that I'm a convict on the lam? Gee, thanks. Chief."

Somehow her laugh didn't quite ring true.

"I guess you're entitled to your secrets," he returned.

"I don't have any secrets. My life is an open, albeit very short, book. A novella at best."

Overhead thunder clapped.

Maggie jumped. She glanced at the sky and then looked toward the gutters on the cottage. "Too bad. I was hoping to get a permit to install a rainwater-harvesting system before it rained."

"Oh, there will be plenty more rain days in the valley." He paused. "A permit, huh? That sounds like someone who's thinking about sticking around."

She pondered his words for a moment. "Maybe."

Suddenly the sky opened up, releasing giant drops that quickly turned into a deluge.

"I better get going." Jake tossed his keys into the air.

Maggie touched his arm, and he glanced down, surprised to see her delicate hand on his sleeve.

"This is a downpour, Jake. Can't you wait until it eases up?"

His brows rose at the concern on her face. "Are you worried about me?"

"I'm speaking as a soil professional. It's very dangerous to drive through a downpour in a region indigenous to flash flooding and mudslides." Her soft brown eyes pleaded with him. "And I know from experience that you don't do dangerous, Chief MacLaughlin," she murmured.

Jack met her unwavering gaze. She was right on both counts. Standing this close to Maggie, surrounded by an intimate curtain of rain, was dangerous all right. Much too dangerous.

He lifted the collar of his shirt. "I'll be fine," he said as he stepped from the porch and straight into the cooling rain.

"Chuck, I'm telling you the woman is hiding something."

The black-and-white collie-shepherd mix opted not to answer, nor did he look up from the metal bowl, where his nose was buried in his dinner.

"We're going to have to ask Sheriff Lawson to

run a background check on Maggie Jones. And while Sam is checking, we'll do a little online search of our own, as well."

Chuck finally looked up, his black eyes round and questioning.

"Oh, don't give me that. It's just a simple precaution. She took a cab from Denver, Chuck. Who does that?"

Rain continued to tap at the window as Jake stirred the simmering Buffalo chili and then replaced the lid on the pot and turned down the flame. He grabbed a sponge and wiped down the stainless steel stove top before sliding cornbread muffins into the oven and setting the timer.

Almost time to eat. It would have been nice to share dinner with someone besides his dog.

For a moment his mind flitted back to Maggie. He quickly dismissed the concerned expression he'd seen on her face as he left her house.

Long ago, he'd resolved himself to being alone. Once a month his solitary life was interrupted when he met his men at the firehouse for training and they put together a meal. Occasionally his father dropped in unannounced, too. Oddly enough, Mack hadn't done much of that in the last few months.

A loud rhythmic series of raps on the back door signaled tonight was one of those visits from his father. Jake smiled as Chuck raced to the door and shoved his whiskers into the screen, whining.

"Jacob," his father called as he pushed the door open. "Quite a storm out there. Hope it stops before the weekend." He shrugged off his yellow rain slicker and ran a hand through his damp hair.

"Hey, Dad. You smelled the chili all the way from your place, huh?"

"Are you cooking?" Mack leaned down and gave Chuck a rubdown. "Yeah, boy, I've missed you, too."

"There's chili in the pot."

Mack stood and looked around. "Oh, I guess you are. But that's not why I'm here. I want to run something by you."

"Sure. Have a seat and maybe Chuck and I can help you with your problem."

"I don't have a problem." Mack eased onto a black leather bar stool and rested his hands on the countertop of the kitchen's island.

"This isn't about the webpage, is it?"

"No." His father waved one of his big hands in the air.

"We're listening." Jake looked down at Chuck, who was staring at the stove. "Pay attention, Chuck."

"It's been over ten years since…" Mack avoided Jake's gaze and ran a hand over the smooth granite counter as he searched for words. "Well, you know..."

Jake nodded. Was this going to be another of his father's speeches about getting back into life? Finding a good woman and providing him with grandchildren? Mack usually tossed in a reminder that Jake was his only son and neither of them was getting any younger.

"I'll be seventy next month."

"Not getting any younger," Jake mumbled.

Mack slammed a hand on the counter. "Exactly."

The buzzer on the oven went off and Jake donned protective mitts before removing the tin of golden corn muffins.

"It's time to get back into the swing of things," Mack continued.

"I've got a date for the Founder's Day supper with Maggie Jones. Does that count?" he asked as he turned off the oven.

"Sure does." Mack cleared his throat. "But I'm actually referring to me. Not you."

Jake froze, and then slowly turned around. "You?"

There was an unmistakable twinkle in his father's eyes as he smiled.

"This is good, Dad. Real good." Jake was genuinely pleased. It had been a long time since his mother passed—in fact, it had been shortly after Jake lost his wife.

"Glad you feel that way," Mack said, his grin becoming wider. "Because I'm thinking of getting married."

"Married?" He stared at his father and groped for words. "Whoa, what's the rush? What about dating?"

"Dating is for people who don't know what they want. I know what I want." Mack narrowed his eyes. "Besides, I wasn't asking for your permission."

Jake grinned. "Right. Right. Just giving you a hard time." He pulled off the mitts. "So that's why you haven't been popping by for dinner. Someone else has been feeding you."

Mack's face flamed. "No comment."

Jake settled on a stool opposite his father and crossed his arms. "Marriage, huh? Who is this mystery woman?"

"You'll know soon enough."

"I'm your son. You can't tell me?"

"You'll know soon enough." Mack met his gaze, his expression solemn. "So you're okay with this, Jacob?"

"Absolutely. Congratulations, Dad."

"Thanks."

"Big step. So what's next? You two going to give me the baby brother I always wanted?"

Mack picked up a towel from the counter and swung it at Jake. "You know, you've been hanging around those fire jockeys too long. You're just a barrel of laughs."

Chuck barked and jumped in a circle, his toenails clicking on the tile floor.

"Now you've done it," Jake said. "I'll have to play fetch with him for an hour to wear him out."

"Your own fault."

"So do you want some chili or not?"

Mack glanced at his watch and stood. "Like to, but she's waiting on me. I have to run. Oh, and keep this under your hat. I just wanted to feel you out first."

"You're sure you can't give me a hint?"

"Nope." He grinned. "She might not even say yes."

"No woman would turn down a MacLaughlin."

"Ha. I wouldn't take that to the bank. But if she does say yes, you'll be my best man, right?"

Jake swallowed the lump in his throat. "You bet."

Mack smiled even wider.

"Come here, big guy." He offered his father a man hug, then stood back. "I'm happy for you."

"Thanks, Jacob. It means a lot that my son supports me."

"Now get going before you get in the doghouse. I'll see you tomorrow at the hardware store."

He clapped his father on the back as they walked to the door.

"Thanks, again, son." Mack slipped his arms into his rain slicker. "I knew I could count on you."

Jake smiled as his father ran through the rain, dodging puddles until he reached his car.

Only then did he walk into his darkened living room and sink to his leather recliner.

Marriage.

He'd been excited for his dad just moments ago when he'd revealed he was seeing someone, but marriage? Jake couldn't imagine his father with someone besides his mom. Thoughts of his petite and unassuming mother filled his mind. She had been the gentle guiding force in their family. He missed her. Jake hung his head, ashamed of his resentful thoughts. *Forgive me, Lord. I am happy for my father.*

After all, it had been ten years. They'd both been alone for a long time. His father's announcement was unexpected, that was all. Being nostalgic was normal.

Seemed like lately the moment he adjusted himself to some new normal, things changed again. As if confirming his internal argument, Maggie Jones's warm brown eyes and her full smile filled his mind.

"Yeah, right," he scoffed as the words tumbled aloud into the empty room. "Me and Maggie. About as likely as my father marrying Bitsy Harmony."

Chapter Five

According to the Colorado State University Extension webpage, the timing was perfect for planting. Maggie leaned into the shovel, turning over a clod of wet soil. It had been two weeks since the last frost, and she was bound and determined to get some vegetables planted.

She'd purchased tomato and pepper plants, as well as the various seeds. Maybe she'd be able to squeeze enough from her budget for a few lavender plants, as well.

"Sphagnum."

Startled, Maggie looked up. "Excuse me?" A tall woman stood at the edge of the yard, inspecting.

Ageless. That was Maggie's immediate impression. Not young, and certainly not old. She wore navy slacks and a powder-blue blouse with a crisp white collar. A handsome woman with a strong jaw and sharp blue eyes, her silver white hair was twisted into a bun that sat dead center on the top of her head.

"Soil needs some sphagnum peat."

"Any opinion on molasses and alfalfa tea fertilizer?" Maggie asked.

The woman walked toward Maggie. "New to me. What you really need is a rototiller."

The woman's attention had moved beyond Maggie to the long row of scraggly rose bushes at the back of the garden.

"What a shame. I remember when they produced some of the loveliest blooms in Paradise."

"You've been here before?"

"Oh, yes. I've lived in Paradise most of my life. Hardly a home I haven't been invited into." A sigh escaped her thin lips. "My grandmother used coffee grounds. Works wonders. You might try that. Mix them into the soil at the base of the plant about once a week."

"I'll give that a try."

The woman's gaze returned to Maggie and she gave a short nod and thrust out her hand. "Bitsy Harmony."

So this was the famous Bitsy Harmony? Using her teeth, Maggie removed a mud-caked glove and took the hand Bitsy offered. The strong, firm grip belied the woman's years.

"Hope you don't mind my stopping by unannounced. I was in the neighborhood. You know Mack MacLaughlin lives right down the street."

"Yes. I heard that."

Bitsy glanced down, as if just realizing she held a pie in her other hand. "Oh, here. This is for you. Peach. We grow fine peaches in Paradise. My pies generally take a ribbon every year."

"That's what everyone tells me. Thank you," Maggie said, removing the other glove. "May I offer you a cup of coffee, or some tea?"

"Tea would be fine. Though I can't stay long. Due back at the office, soon." Bitsy chuckled. "The sheriff thinks I'm running errands."

"You work for the sheriff?" Maggie asked as she took the foil-covered pie tin.

"Administrative secretary for the Paradise Sheriff's Department. That means I do everything except carry a sidearm."

"I see," Maggie said, though she didn't. The real question was why was Bitsy Harmony at her home on a Tuesday morning?

As Bitsy followed Maggie around to the side of the house, she paused to give the rest of the yard a once-over. "I'll bring you some grape hyacinth next time I come. Makes a nice border and brightens up the scenery."

"Muscari armeniacum. That would be wonderful. Thank you."

"Heard you were a professional. That must be the scientific name for grape hyacinth?"

"It is." Maggie smiled as she slipped off her boots.

"Thought so. You're a Colorado native?" Bitsy asked.

"Yes. Denver," Maggie answered, holding the screen for the older woman.

Bitsy nodded approval at the answer. As they entered the small home she glanced around, pausing to eye the pale gray walls, white beadboard wainscoting and polished wood floors. "Haven't been inside the cottage in years. It's lovely."

"Thank you. That would be my cousin Susan's work." Maggie turned on the burner under the kettle and took two mugs down from the cupboard. She prepared a tray and placed it on the table.

"Not much furniture," Bitsy noted.

"Enough for me," Maggie said.

"I've got some pieces in storage that are collecting dust."

"That's awfully nice of you, but I'm not even certain I'm staying."

"Oh, you're staying."

"Excuse me?" Maggie turned to meet Bitsy's serious gaze.

"I've got a feeling about you and I can't say I'm wrong once I get a feeling."

"Do you get these feelings often?" she asked.

"Last time was Dr. Ben Rogers, and he's still here. Married with twins now."

Maggie swallowed a retort, and instead turned up the flame under the teapot.

"That's some stove," Bitsy continued. "Looks like it will do everything, except the dishes."

Maggie laughed at Bitsy's assessment of the stainless steel giant that boasted a regular oven, a convection oven and a griddle next to eight gas burners. "Susan says she bought it during her Food Network phase."

"Do you cook?"

"I get by," Maggie said, unwilling to verbalize aloud that her skills in the kitchen were rudimentary on a good day.

"Bake?"

"No."

"Maybe I could show you how to bake a pie."

"Really?"

Bitsy opened an oven door and peeked inside. "Sure. Nothing to it. Most people overthink when it comes to pies. 'Course, you know that it's the surest way to a man's affection."

Once again, an appropriate response evaded Maggie.

The oven door slammed shut and Bitsy faced Maggie. "So what do you think of Jake?"

"Jake?"

"Jacob MacLaughlin Junior."

"I, um… He's nice."

"Nice? That's how you describe a spring day in Paradise."

Maggie blinked at the words, but Bitsy simply forged on.

"Jake MacLaughlin is good man. Oh, he's not perfect, mind you. Carries a burden that isn't his to carry. Set in his ways. Been on his own far too long. I imagine some prayers and the right woman could change all that, and I'm working on both." She raised her brows and looked Maggie up and down in silent assessment.

Stunned, all Maggie could do was return a weak smile, as the kettle began its shrill whistle, cutting off Bitsy's next words.

"So, I'd like you to give Jake a chance.

Maggie's eyes widened as she reached for a pot holder. "Could you run that by me again?"

"Paradise is a splendid little town, don't you think?"

"Yes, yes," she agreed, pouring the steaming water into the mugs.

"But we sadly lack a choice population of unmarried females under the age of sixty-five."

"I see" was all Maggie could come up with as she returned the kettle to the stove.

"I knew you would." Bitsy selected a tea bag and placed it in her mug. "So you'll keep an open mind?"

"About what?"

Bitsy shot Maggie a look clearly accusing her of not paying attention. "Jake."

"You understand that we hardly know each other and the Founder's Day thing isn't a date or anything."

"I understand." Steely blue eyes pinned her with a determined gaze. "But you'll give him a chance?"

Capitulation was the only option. "Yes. Okay, I'll do that."

Without skipping a beat, Bitsy sipped her tea, a satisfied smile on her face. "Now about that garden. You'll find the soil around here difficult but not impossible. Quality peat moss will loosen things up. At least six bags for a garden that size. Then you'll need a good fertilizer with nitrogen, phosphorous and potash. And a rototiller. I'll have to get a rototiller over here. They rent them out at the hardware store."

"Really. That's not necessary."

"I know Mack real well. I'll have one here tomorrow. Morning work for you?"

"Morning?" Maggie scrambled for an answer. "Um, I suppose I could make it work. Thank you."

"What are you doing tomorrow night?" Bitsy asked.

Her mind raced, as prickles of concern washed over her. "Nothing… Why do you ask?"

"I'll have your Aunt Betty pick you up. The

Paradise Ladies Auxiliary meets at my house on Wednesday nights."

"But..."

"Community involvement will look good on your résumé, especially to the school board."

Maggie's jaw dropped. "How did you know?"

Bitsy smiled serenely and sipped her tea. She slowly placed the mug on the table. "This is Paradise. One thing you'll find out pretty quick is that around here there's no such thing as a stranger. If you came here for quiet, fine. If you came here for privacy, well, good luck."

Leaning back in her chair, Maggie paused to absorb the woman's words. What had she gotten herself into?

Maggie's ears perked and she straightened from the counter, where she had been watching the coffee drip—much too slowly—into the glass carafe. Was that a knock? She glanced at the clock as the doorbell rang. It was 7:00 a.m.

Padding barefoot across the living room, she tiptoed to the peephole. Jake? Now what crime had she committed? Maggie glanced down at her clothes. Well, at least they weren't wrinkled. Much.

She removed the chain lock and opened the door. Jake MacLaughlin stood bright-eyed on her porch, in jeans and a crisp denim shirt, rolled up at the sleeves. An enthusiastic black-and-white dog sat eagerly at his feet.

"Jake? Is everything okay?"

"Sure. Delivering the rototiller. It's in my truck. Mack said you wanted it here early."

"Mack? But Bitsy is the one who…" She shook her head. "Well, never mind. Thank you for bringing it by."

"Do I smell coffee?" he asked.

"Yes. Would you like a cup?"

"Now there's a hearty invitation."

"Sorry." She put on a smile though she was still unconvinced that inviting Jake into her home was a bright idea. "May I offer you a cup of freshly brewed coffee, Chief MacLaughlin?"

"Don't mind if I do."

Maggie glanced at the dog. "Who's your friend?"

"This is Chuck."

She nodded and opened the screen. "Come on in."

"Chuck. Stay."

The dog whined, but obeyed.

"Nice place," Jake observed as he followed her into the kitchen.

"All Susan's doing. She got the domestic gene."

"What are you working on?" he asked.

Across from a small floral sofa and chair in the living room, an oak table was covered with newspaper and on top were a metal toolbox and an array of tools. A small engine sat in the middle of the chaos.

"Oh, that's the engine from a garden fountain. One of the ladies from the auxiliary brought it in and I told her I'd see what I could do."

Jake looked at the project from all angles. "You know, most women knit or sew or bake cookies in their spare time."

"I'm not most women," she said as she continued to move toward the kitchen.

"I noticed."

She gestured to one of the mismatched chairs positioned around a small nook table tucked beneath a bay window. "A little early for insults, isn't it?"

He slid into the chair. "That wasn't an insult. Being different is good."

"Not in my experience," she muttered.

Maggie pulled another mug from the cupboard as the coffeepot sputtered the last drops into the carafe.

"So, you met Bitsy?" he asked.

"You mean, Hurricane Harmony?"

Jake laughed. "That's Bitsy."

"We met yesterday. I'm still picking up the pieces."

"No doubt."

"The interesting thing is that while I saw it coming—" Maggie shook her head "—I didn't have a clue how to stop it or even get out of the way."

"Don't let her play that game too often or before you know it she'll have you signed up for every committee in Paradise and in her free time she'll manage your personal life."

Maggie could only sigh as she poured the coffee. "Cream? Sugar?"

"Black, please. And I'm not kidding."

"I know you aren't. It would have been good to have this information before she blew past."

"You joined the auxiliary."

She nodded and handed him a mug.

Jake clucked his tongue. "I can't help you now."

"As usual, my own fault."

He sipped his coffee. "Good coffee."

"Don't look so surprised." She pulled open a cupboard and pointed to several boxes. "Did you want a toaster pastry with that?"

"Uh, no, I'll pass. Thank you."

Maggie leaned against the counter and eyed him. "Do you always make deliveries for the hardware store," she asked.

"No, we've got a guy who does that. There was some sort of overbooking glitch. We're computerized, so I don't know how it happened. But my dad asked me to help out."

"Nice of you."

"Part of the job." He shrugged. "You know how to run a rototiller?"

"No, however I am very big on manuals."

"I bet you are—only it doesn't come with a manual."

"Oh. Well, I'll figure it out."

He looked out the window at the yard. "That's a big project. I'm happy to help."

"I don't want to bother you," she said.

"I'm here. Allow me to help."

"But—"

"I'll get the tiller and gasoline can from my truck." He pulled keys out of his pocket. "Could you do a walk-through for any sticks, or rocks or anything else that might be in the yard, before I come through with the tiller?"

"Of course."

Maggie slipped an old sweatshirt over her head before she pushed open the side door and stepped into the yard.

A perfect Colorado morning. Perfect for tilling after the recent rain. Or possibly a little too wet. This might prove to be a messy job.

She tied the laces on her boots and grabbed a trash bag, and began to walk through the garden area, poking at the dirt with a stick and carefully inspecting the mud.

Jake appeared, pushing the rototiller, with Chuck at his side.

"Mind if Chuck watches?"

"No, of course not. Would he like a cup of coffee, too?"

Jake laughed. "He's fine, though we appreciate the hospitality." He put on his safety glasses, rolled down his sleeves and pulled on gloves before yanking on the tiller cord. The machine roared to life.

Maggie stepped back as he directed the tiller into the area she had just cleared. He steered the turning blades into the soil, making parallel passes through the garden.

Halfway across the plot, as she stooped down to pick up a stick, Maggie realized something had struck her between the shoulder blades. She twisted her sweatshirt around.

Dirt.

She glanced over at Jake but his concentration remained fixed on the ground and the task at hand.

Probably an accident.

Maggie proceeded down the next row, stopping after a moment to pick up a large rock. A clod of moist dirt slapped her yet again, this time landing right on the seat of jeans. She narrowed her eyes at Jake.

Nothing.

When it happened a third time she grabbed a clump of soil and threw it in Jake's general direction.

"What're you doing?" he yelled above the roar of the tiller.

"Sorry. Accident."

A few minutes later, surprise made her shoot straight up as a blob of mud slapped her backside.

Jake must have felt her glaring, because he turned and angled his head, assessing the situation. His face wore a puzzled expression.

Maggie scooped up a good chunk of dirt and carefully tossed it at him. The clod landed squarely on his shirtsleeve.

Jake turned off the tiller. He patiently shook the soil off the sleeve of his once-pristine shirt. "What are you doing?"

"You're throwing dirt at me." She turned to show him the back of her shirt and jeans.

Though he wasn't laughing his amber eyes were bright with amusement. "Not me, it's the tiller."

"Well, your tiller is shooting dirt and hitting my backside."

"I suppose I could aim a little better." He bent down and picked up a fresh piece of wet soil, focused and threw it. The chunk landed on her arm.

"Aim better? Seriously?" She responded by selecting a generous blob of mud and formed the mess into a ball.

"Wait. No. Maggie." Jake took a step backward. "Don't even think—"

She wound up like a pitcher on the mound and released. The ball of mud splattered across

Jake's chest, bits decorating his chin. Maggie stood back and admired her handiwork.

The morning air was quiet as Jake swiped at his chin with the back of his hand. Slowly, and with the utmost deliberation, he used two hands to gather an impressive amount of dirt. Maggie could only be grateful his handfuls weren't nearly as wet as hers had been.

He winked, his attention completely upon Maggie. She realized much too late that she might have underestimated him.

Maggie cringed and narrowed her eyes as Jake targeted her feet. She jumped back as the dirt ball landed hard and exploded.

With a raised finger, Jake scratched a point on an invisible chalkboard in the air.

"Truce?" he asked, with an engaging smile that lit up his face.

She dragged her gaze from his smile, paused and considered the offer, scanning his clothing, then hers. "Truce," she agreed, trying to keep a straight face.

Nodding with satisfaction, he yanked on the tiller's start cord, bringing the machine back to life, and began to turn over the soil in parallel rows.

She was covered with dirt and yet all she could do was smile. Truce, he'd said. But could she trust him?

Maggie bit her lip, vowing to keep a watchful eye on Jake MacLaughlin.

Jake grinned at his reflection in the mirror and wiped another streak of mud off his face. He had to give Maggie credit, she was a good shot. His chin and neck were peppered with mud. She was a good sport, as well. He hadn't expected that. And he hadn't had that much fun in a long time, either.

When he came out of the restroom, there was peach pie dished and waiting for him in the cozy kitchen. Maggie had changed clothes and was drying dishes by hand.

Jake smiled. "That pie for me?"

"Yes. You certainly earned it. Despite the mud bath, I am very appreciative of your help."

"My pleasure."

"What do you want with that? Iced tea? Coffee?"

"Have any milk?"

"Sure." She poured a glass for him.

He bit into the pie and savored the flavors. "Whoa. This tastes like Bitsy Harmony's pie."

"It is Bitsy's."

His head jerked back. "Bitsy gave you a pie?"

"Yes."

"You're on her good side already."

"I got the feeling it was more like she was trying to get on my good side."

"You're probably right." He frowned, trying

to put the pieces together. One thing was clear. He'd been outsmarted by Mack and Bitsy. Yep. They'd gotten him to deliver the rototiller.

Jake met Maggie's gaze and she smiled, touching something deep inside him.

He picked up the fork. Lucky for them he didn't mind being hoodwinked. This time.

"Aren't you having any pie?" he asked Maggie. "You worked as hard as I did."

She cut herself a small piece and stood at the counter.

"I don't bite."

Maggie slid her plate onto the table and pulled out the chair across from him.

"Looks like you missed a spot."

"Hmm?"

Jake picked up a napkin and wiped a trace of mud off the back of her hand.

"Thanks."

He glanced pointedly at the white band of skin on her ring finger. "Lose a ring?"

"Engagement ring."

His eyes rounded in surprise. Something almost like jealousy stirred inside of him. "You were engaged? Pretty recent?"

Maggie took a deep breath. "Yes." She bit her lip. "I was supposed to get married this weekend."

"This weekend?" The air whooshed from his lungs as realization hit. "That's why you took a cab from Denver."

She nodded slowly.

"A runaway bride? Mind if I ask what happened?"

"I realized at the last minute that I was going along for the ride to make everyone happy—everyone but myself." She swallowed hard. "And he didn't love me."

"I'm sorry, Maggie," Jake said.

He searched her eyes, seeing the pain. "Better you realized before the wedding, right?"

She met his gaze. "Of course, but I'm not upset about the breakup. Actually I'm relieved about that. I'm upset that I spent so many years trying to please others instead of myself."

"Take my advice, sometimes all you can do is make peace with the past and move on."

"I'm still working on that part."

The ringing of a phone interrupted the silence that stretched between them.

"Your phone?"

Maggie turned around and grabbed her cell from the counter. "Hello? Yes. This is Margaret Jones."

A tiny gasp escaped her lips and her brown eyes lit up.

"Thank you so much. Yes. I will. Absolutely. I'll see you tomorrow, then."

Jake raised his brows in question. "Good news?"

"That was the county school board. They got

my résumé and they want me to come in for an interview tomorrow."

"There's a job opening? How did you find out about it?"

"Beck told me. It's a temporary teaching position at the high school. I emailed my résumé over yesterday." The excitement that bubbled over was contagious.

"And the college professor from Denver would consider teaching at a high school in Paradise?"

"Of course."

Of course.

"That's great. Congratulations, Maggie."

"I don't have the job yet."

"Oh, I'll be praying."

"Will you?" she asked, her head tilted so her ponytail hung askew.

"Sure will."

Maggie staying in Paradise? He wrapped his mind around the idea, liking it more and more. Oh, yeah. He'd be praying.

He met her gaze and smiled, then looked away, forcing himself to concentrate on the pie instead of the woman across the table from him, because in a stunning instant he realized that he'd been right all along. Maggie Jones held the power to do some serious damage to his heart and that fact rocked him.

Chapter Six

Bells chimed as Maggie pushed open the door to the Hair Emporium on Main Street. Immediately the buzz of conversations came to a sudden halt and whiplash moved through the shop like the wave at a football game.

Women popped their heads out from beneath the dryer hoods and craned their necks. At a far sink, a technician shampooing someone's hair peeked around a large woman with pink sponge rollers in an effort to assess Maggie. A manicurist seated against the wall swiped fuchsia enamel across a patron's nail and looked up and over her bifocals. All eyes were focused on the door.

The pungent and unmistakable scent of a perm in progress wrapped itself around Maggie's throat and tightened. She swallowed before taking a tentative step into the room. *Where was Susan?*

From across the busy shop, a petite woman

in a white lab coat moved through the activity toward Maggie.

Self-confidence.

And this woman owned it. Her heels clicked on the linoleum as she approached. The name *Sally-Anne* was stitched in black on the pocket of her pristine jacket. Her glossy black hair framed her face in a short, banged bob that swung back and then forth as she propelled her lithe frame forward.

Sally-Anne's age seemed impossible to determine—somewhere between forty and…forty? The woman was flawless, from her perfect makeup to her impeccable French manicured fingertips.

"Maggie Jones." She gave a short nod. "Sally-Anne."

"How did you know who I am?"

Sally-Anne smiled and pointed to the newspaper on the counter. "You've made the front page. Again. Twice in less than seven days."

"I didn't realize anyone was counting."

"Welcome to Paradise." She gestured with a wave of her arm, toward the window of the shop. "And you've met Chief MacLaughlin."

"Yes, but…" Panic hit Maggie. Surely the woman didn't think… "Those fires were accidents," she finally said.

"I'm sure they were." The other woman offered an indulgent smile as she moved behind the counter and scanned her computer screen. "What can we do for you today? I don't see any notes next to your appointment," Sally-Anne said.

Maggie gripped the small clutch purse in her hands tightly and searched out the window, hoping to spot Susan or her little red car. "My cousin is supposed to meet me here. Maybe I should reschedule."

"Nonsense. We're booked solid due to the Founder's Day events on Saturday."

"Okay, then, I guess a trim would be good." She pushed a loose lock of hair behind her ears.

"A trim?" Sally-Anne stepped from behind the counter and circled Maggie.

Maggie heard the acute disappointment in the woman's tone.

She reached out a hand to inspect a strand of Maggie's hair. Then she fingered another strand and rubbed it between her fingers. Raising red-framed glasses from the chain around her neck onto her nose, Sally-Anne examined the ends of Maggie's hair, all the while uttering dispiriting noises of assessment under her breath.

Behind them the door burst open, setting the bells into a frenzy of noise. *Susan.* The cavalry had arrived.

"Style and cut and low lights. I brought a picture." Susan handed Sally-Anne a page torn from a magazine, then glanced at herself in the mirror behind the front counter and adjusted the Peter Pan collar on her white silk blouse.

"Hmm." Narrowing her eyes, Sally-Anne analyzed the photo for a moment before holding the paper next to Maggie's face. Then she turned to Susan. "Deep conditioning is critical. The follicles have been seriously neglected."

Neglected follicles. The accusation stabbed at Maggie's already dismal self-esteem.

"That will be fine," Susan said. "We want her to dazzle. She's going to the supper with Jake, you know."

Maggie's eyes widened when Sally-Anne perked up, and her jaw sagged in surprise.

"You have a date with our Jake?"

A buzz started through the shop. Someone under the dryer whispered loudly to the woman seated next to her. "Late with Jake?"

"No. A date with Jake," her dryer partner corrected.

Maggie cringed. "Not exactly a date," she said. "I won him."

"Oh, it was you. I heard a Margaret won. I thought it was a woman at the retirement home."

"Maggie. Margaret. I'm named after my grandmother."

"Two hundred tickets, was it?"

Maggie swallowed. "One hundred and forty-seven. Actually Susan bought the tickets."

"I thought we were playing fair," Sally-Anne said.

"Oh, come on now," Susan responded. "You, of all people, realize that rules are out the window when it comes to firemen.

"Humph." Sally-Anne dusted off the first throne and ushered Maggie to sit on the black leather upholstery. She snapped black latex gloves onto her hands. Then she carefully mixed tubes of color into a black bowl and began to paint sections of Maggie's hair with a brush, before carefully folding each section in foil.

"Would you like something to drink while your hair processes?" Sally-Anne asked as she rolled the gloves off her hands.

"No. I'm fine, thanks." Maggie sat quietly watching the other women in the shop and the procedures going on with interest. Across the room, Susan sat in a reclining chair enjoying a pedicure and a cappuccino.

Sally-Anne came over to Maggie's chair at intervals and peeked inside the foil on her head, then nodded her approval and left again. When a buzzer signaled the color was done, Maggie was turned over to a technician at the shampoo sinks.

"The works," Sally-Anne commanded. "Give her the deep conditioning treatment, as well."

Once shampoo and deep conditioning were

complete, a towel-headed Maggie was moved to yet another chair.

"Very nice," Sally-Anne observed, combing out Maggie's hair. "Wear a hat outside from now on. The Colorado sun is ruthless, especially at this elevation."

Maggie nodded at the instructions.

"When was your last salon visit?"

"Oh, this is my first time at a salon."

Sally-Anne choked. "Well, I hope it won't be your last."

"No," Maggie murmured. She kept her eyes fixed on the laces of her sneakers as they peeked out from beneath the cape.

"You're staying with the Joneses?"

"I'm staying at Susan's cottage."

"And you'll be teaching at the high school in the fall?"

Maggie's head jerked back. "How did you know about the job? I haven't even interviewed yet."

With a fingertip, Sally-Anne tilted Maggie's head to the left. "Try not to move or you'll end up with a très chic pixie cut."

"But—"

"This is Paradise. The grapevine is faster than a text message."

"Terrific."

"How long have you known Jake?" she inquired as her thin, tapered, silver scissors snipped, snipped, snipped.

"Seven days."

She stopped cutting. "Seven days?" Sally-Anne gave Maggie an intense scrutiny in the mirror. "And you won a date with two hundred tickets?"

"One hundred and forty-seven, and it was Susan."

The scissors began again. Sally-Anne moved around Maggie, her eyes narrowed and her brows knit in thought as she worked.

A few minutes later the snipping stopped once more.

"He's widowed, you know."

The shoulders of the black plastic cape rustled as Maggie straightened in the chair. She met Sally's eyes in the mirror.

"Our chief is a tortured soul."

"I didn't know," Maggie murmured.

The blow dryer began, its white noise blocking out everything else.

Jake was widowed? Maggie sat stunned at the information. The pain she'd read in his eyes was real. He had loved and suffered the worst imaginable loss. Didn't she feel like a horrible human being for how she'd jumped to so very many thoughtless conclusions about the man?

Oh, Lord, please forgive me and my big mouth. I'll be nicer to Jake from now on.

If only he wouldn't goad her. He seemed to know how to push all her buttons and he enjoyed doing it, too.

Sally-Anne circled the chair, repositioning Maggie's head with a touch of her hand.

"What do you think?" Sally-Anne asked.

Maggie looked up in time to see Susan's grinning face reflected in the mirror.

"You look amazing, Mags."

With a small hand mirror, Maggie examined herself from several angles. Sally Anne was a gifted stylist. The cut flattered. Strands of caramel and golden brown hair danced on her shoulders, with wispy layers and bangs framing her face. Oh, yes. She had to admit the change was amazing.

"Do you think I can get it to do this by myself?"

"Of course. Let me recommend a line of shampoo, conditioner and style extender. Also a nice ceramic brush." Sally-Anne reached for the supplies and placed them on the counter.

The register sang joyfully, as it tallied up the purchases. Maggie gulped as her budget flatlined. Except when she looked at the receipt she'd only been charged for the brush, and hair products.

"This is incorrect. You undercharged me," she said.

Sally-Anne waved a hand in dismissal. "Professional courtesy. Your cousin is a member of the Paradise Small Business Association with me. Besides, your hair is the best word-of-mouth advertisement I could ever hope for."

"Thank you, so much," Maggie said.

"Thank you. Remember a good haircut is like a good marriage. You do your part, and I do mine."

"I'm not sure I can live up to my end of this… marriage. I haven't looked this good in my entire life." Maggie stared at herself in the mirror behind the counter. She swung her head and the layers moved and then settled in attractive disarray.

"Don't be so hard on yourself. You had the basic resources to start with."

"No. It's all you, Sally-Anne. You're an artist."

Sally-Anne purred. "Now I know why Jake likes you. You're nice, even if you are breaking the heart of every woman in Paradise who is in love with Jake MacLaughlin."

"No. No. Jake and I… He doesn't."

"No worries. I didn't say this would stop the rest of us from trying."

Maggie couldn't resist a laugh.

"See you at the supper," Sally-Anne said, as she handed a hot pink shopping bag to Maggie. "Oh, and here's a coupon for fifty percent off a manicure."

Instinctively Maggie curled her nails into

her palms. They were a mess from yard work. "Thank you."

"Are we still on for lunch?" Susan asked as she linked her arm through Maggie's. "My treat."

"Sure."

"Patti Jo's?"

"Sounds good."

Maggie and Susan strolled down Main Street to the corner, where the red doors of Patti Jo's Café and Bakery welcomed them. When Susan opened the door, Aunt Betty stood on the other side.

"Mother," Susan said. "Are you getting off work?"

"Lunch break. I saw you two coming down the street through the window. May I join you?"

"Of course," Susan said.

"Maggie." Aunt Betty's eyes popped wide. "Your hair. I don't think I've ever seen you without a ponytail. You've worn a ponytail since you were a little girl. You look so different."

"Is that good?"

Aunt Betty cocked her head and stared at her. "I think it's good, but Maggie, you're a beautiful woman. Are you ready for that?"

"What do you mean, Aunt B?"

"You might not be prepared for the attention you'll be getting."

"Mom is telling you to get used to it, Mags. Life as you know it is about to change."

"That's a stretch." Maggie fingered her bangs. "But, I guess I never realized how bad I looked before."

"You never looked bad. Simply a case of hidden potential," Susan said.

They'd only barely slid into a high-backed booth when Susan's phone trilled. She dug in her leather satchel and pulled out her cell. "Excuse me. I'm going to slip outside and take this."

Maggie's gaze wandered around the room, taking in the black-and-white tiled floor, the cute retro-style cherry-red and aluminum tables and booths. "How long have you worked here, Aunt B?"

"I only work in the spring and summer. It's very busy when the tourists hit town and I like having a little extra cash of my own to put away for the holidays."

Susan appeared back at the table. "I'm so sorry. A shipment just arrived and I've got to deal with the vendor. With the Founder's Day supper I've got all sorts of merchandise I have to get on display." She looked at Maggie. "Mom will take good care of you, Maggie.

Aunt Betty patted Maggie's hand. "It's okay, Susan. We'll be fine."

"I'll stop by Saturday morning to help you dress for the parade."

"I can dress myself, you know," Maggie said.

"I'll see you Saturday morning." Susan waved and headed for the door.

"Susan..."

The waitress appeared at their table, cutting off Maggie's opportunity to protest.

"What do you recommend, Aunt Betty?"

"The chicken Caesar wraps. Best in town."

Maggie smiled at the young redheaded waitress. "Two wraps then."

"And to drink?"

"Iced tea, please," Maggie said.

Her aunt handed the menus to the teenage server. "I'll have the same. Oh, and Julia, have you met my niece, Maggie?"

The girl smiled. "No, but I heard about you."

"It wasn't my fault!"

"Excuse me? Oh, I meant Beck. He told me that he works for you. He actually talks about you a lot."

"You're a friend of Beck's?"

The teen blushed. "Yes. He's really brilliant, isn't he?"

"Yes. All that and something else," Maggie agreed. "Nice to meet you, Julia."

"You, too."

"Wow," Maggie said as Julia walked away, a dreamy smile on her face. "Can you say 'crush'?"

"You think so?"

"For sure, Aunt B."

"Young love."

"Beck has tunnel vision. He probably has no clue."

"Speaking of romance, Maggie, how are you doing?"

"Me? Romance?" Maggie looked up from the dessert menu. "What do you mean?"

"This Saturday is the date you would have been getting married."

"I know. My bank account reminded me this morning."

"Apparently you aren't bemoaning the loss."

"Only the dent on my savings after I sent a check to my parents for all the deposits they lost."

"Oh, Maggie, you reimbursed your parents?"

"I was the one who ran."

"Hmm." Aunt Betty shot a stern frown at Maggie. "I was under the impression that the engagement and arrangements were your parents' idea."

"I'm thirty-two years old. I should have put my foot down before everything got out of control. And it was way out of control, believe me." She took a small drink of water. "Anyhow. That's behind me now."

"Is it? Have you talked to your parents since you left?"

"No. I'm avoiding another conversation, as is my 'head in the sand' way."

"Maggie, you need to check in with them."

"I will. Sunday is Father's Day. I'd planned to call then."

Maggie folded and unfolded her napkin. "Aunt B, why is it I'm so different from my parents? Do you think maybe I was switched at birth?"

Aunt Betty chuckled. "I have often had similar thoughts about your Uncle Bob."

"Uncle Bob? Why?"

"He and your father are so different."

Maggie considered her words. "I never thought about it before, but you're absolutely right."

"Have you ever wondered how we live comfortably in Paradise on the income from a fix-it shop in a town of less than two thousand?"

"Well, come to think of it..."

"Your Uncle Bob is as smart as your father. Not book smart yet smart nonetheless. He simply expresses it differently. Actually, you're a lot like him. Years ago Bob sold one of his fix-it shop projects to a big company in Denver." Betty leaned closer and whispered. "He made a small fortune, Maggie, enough to allow him to fiddle happily with his projects for the rest of his life and not worry about the bills."

Maggie's eyes widened.

"So the fix-it shop is a front?"

Aunt Betty laughed again. "I guess you could say that. He loves that shop dearly."

"I don't blame him."

"You're like Bob. Smart, but in a different way

than most people. You both see the world differently. Don't despise what God has given you, dear. You're different. Period. He made you that way for a reason. There's no condemnation in Him. Be proud. After all, there's only one Maggie Jones, and I think she's pretty wonderful."

Warmth flooded Maggie. She reached out and grasped her aunt's hands.

"Thank you, Aunt B. I needed to hear that."

"Good. And you know, Maggie, the future looks very promising for you, here in Paradise. You're a new committee member of the Paradise Ladies Auxiliary.

"One step at a time, Aunt B. "I've only attended one meeting."

"Trust me. You are a new member and you'll soon be a teacher at our high school."

"I have to interview first. Besides, I don't even know who the other candidates are."

"Maggie, you've got better qualifications than anyone working at that school." She paused. "Actually, I don't think there are any other applicants."

"That's odd."

"No, that's Paradise. We're a vacation destination. Not many folks live here year-round. Keep in mind that all you have to do is stay out of trouble and you're in."

"You're not the first person to say that." Maggie shook her head. "You know, I don't go looking for trouble. For some reason it just sort of finds me."

Aunt Betty smiled. "I know, dear. Maybe you could try to be more alert."

"I will." Maggie nodded. "Um, Aunt B?"

"Yes, dear?"

"What exactly does a committee member on the Paradise Ladies Auxiliary do?"

"Why, whatever Bitsy tells you to do."

"I was afraid of that."

Her aunt laughed.

"Isn't that Maggie Jones?" Duffy said as he shoved another bag of groceries into the fire truck.

"Huh? Where?" Jake picked up a twelve-pack of soda and glanced around. His gaze took in the Pay 'n Pak they'd just come out of, and moved down the street. "I don't see her."

"Over there in the window of Patti Jo's, with Mrs. Jones."

Jake turned around. "I can't tell. They're sitting in that high booth."

"When she stood up a minute ago, I could see her.

"All I can see is the top of that woman's head and there isn't a ponytail."

"I'm telling you, that's Maggie."

"Duff, you need glasses."

"Chief, I already wear glasses."

"Why don't we go get a couple dozen cookies and find out?" Jake said.

"Cinnamon oatmeal raisin?"

"Chocolate chip."

"I'm not going with you for chocolate chip," Duffy returned.

Jake pulled the keys from his pocket and tossed them in the air. Caught off guard, Duffy struggled to catch them.

"Then you can wait here," Jake said.

"No way. I think Maggie likes me. I'm not letting you cut into my territory, either."

"Dream on. The only female in your future is a dalmatian. And for your information, Maggie and I are strictly friends."

"Ha!" Duffy crowed, struggling to keep up with Jake's long strides. "That's a good thing, because you two have nothing in common. I never met two more opposite people."

Jake stopped walking and glared at Duffy. "What are you talking about?"

"You and Maggie. She's about as laid-back as they come."

"So?"

"Well, you're, uh…not."

"What's that supposed to mean?"

"No offense, Chief, but you're kind of tense."

"I'm not tense. I just like things…structured.

Jake started walking again.

"Did you know she's into plants and bees and stuff? She wants to open an organic nursery."

"How is it you know so much about her?" Jake asked, irritation mounting to an all-time high.

"She told me."

"When did you and Maggie have the opportunity to engage in such a deep conversation?"

"When I took her report."

Jake snorted. "Opposites can complement each other," he muttered.

"Are you telling me you're staking claim here, Chief?"

"No."

"Sure sounds that way to me."

"I told you. Maggie and I are friends. Period." Jake pulled open the door to Patti Jo's and Duffy smoothly slid into the café ahead of him.

"Don't turn around, Duff. Play it cool for once, will you, please?"

"I can do subtle.

"Uh-huh."

"Watch me." He stood stiffly at the counter. "Two dozen cinnamon oatmeal raisin, please."

"Make that one dozen and a dozen chocolate chip," Jake said.

"You get an extra cookie for every dozen," the young redhead at the cash register informed them.

Jake narrowed his eyes to read her name tag. Tiny print. Maybe he was the one who needed glasses. "Hey, great, Julia. Make them chocolate chip."

She nodded.

"Oh, and could you do me a favor?" he asked.

"Sure."

He leaned against the glass and lowered his voice. "Could you tell me if that's Betty Jones and her niece in that booth?" He gave a nod of his head in the direction of the window.

"Yes, sir. Mrs. Jones and her niece, Maggie."

"Told you so," Duffy said. "You take care of the bill. I'm going to go say hello."

"Wait a—"

"That's twelve dollars, sir."

Jake tossed a ten and a five on the counter. "Keep the change." He grabbed the bag and swiveled around to follow Duffy to the booth.

"Duffy and Jake. What are you boys up to?" Betty Jones greeted them with a smile.

"Doing a little grocery shopping for the fire station," Duffy said.

The woman with Betty turned away from the window, the layers of her hair caressing her head as she moved.

"Maggie?" Jake choked.

"Told you," Duffy said under his breath, with an elbow to Jake's side.

"Your hair," he breathed.

"She had it done at the Emporium. Doesn't she look nice?" Aunt Betty interjected.

"Man, I'll say," said Duffy. "You look sort of exotic with those bangs. Right, Chief?"

A slight pink tinged Maggie's cheeks.

"You look good, Maggie," Jake said.

"Thank you," she murmured.

"Going to the parade?" Duffy asked.

"Yes. Susan asked me to help her hand out flyers for the Paradise Ladies Auxiliary," Maggie said.

"Oh, brother. What's Bitsy selling now?" Jake asked.

"I have no idea. We'll have to wait and see," Maggie returned with a grin.

"I'll take whatever you're selling," Duffy interjected.

Jake shook his head. Yeah. That was subtle.

"Be sure to look for the fire department in the parade. We always ride the vintage pumper and pass out plastic fire hats to the kids. They love us. Right, Chief?"

"Yeah. Right."

Jake was still adjusting to the new Maggie in front of him. Sure she looked great, but he liked the old Maggie, as well.

This whole do-over-Maggie thing must have been Susan's idea. Susan had a new project every year. Now thanks to her, Maggie would be beating men off with a stick at the supper for sure.

Jake released a frustrated breath. Nope, he didn't like that thought one bit.

Chapter Seven

Jake's hand touched the small of Maggie's back as he led her toward the huge tent covering the park's grassy knoll. Overhead the sky was clear and the trees twinkled with tiny white lights. As they crossed the lawn the scent of summer flowers and pine floated on the faint breeze. The soft crooning of a saxophone called their names, welcoming them to Paradise's biggest event of the year.

Maggie shivered in anticipation.

"Cold?" Jake asked.

"No," she murmured. Not cold, simply giddy with excitement. The Founder's Day event might be something Jake took for granted, but to Maggie this was more than special. After all she was the bookworm who never even attended her high school prom. Tonight she was making up for the lapses in her history.

Inside the tent the space had been transformed,

becoming a glittery paradise. More tiny lights crisscrossed across the high ceiling. The subdued lighting served to enhance the dreamy atmosphere.

Long dining tables covered with white linen tablecloths filled a corner of the tent. Folding chairs were elegantly disguised with white slipcovers. Each table held a scattering of golden glitter and a centerpiece of yellow blooms: tulips, peonies, lilacs, lily of the valley and daisies.

Across the room and against the wall, an endless buffet table barely contained its overflowing bounty. Tiny canapés, fresh shrimp, bowls of salsa with red and blue chips and other appetizers started the feast, which continued to the far end of the buffet, finishing with a lavish array of desserts. A beverage bar occupied the last bit of space at the end.

A small stage dominated the rest of the tent with chairs casually placed around the area. An old-fashioned four-piece band was beginning a set, and already several couples were lured to the stage, swaying as the musicians played familiar melodies from bygone eras.

Maggie softly hummed to the music.

Jake's breath tickled her ear. "You sing, too?"

"Humming. That's what the tone-deaf do. They hum."

He laughed. "I'll have to keep that in mind.

I've been advised not to sing loudly at church anymore. It frightens young children."

She chuckled.

As they stood listening to the band, a stream of Paradise's citizens stopped to say hello to the chief and meet Maggie.

"They're all curious about you," Jake said.

"That's because I've been on the front page of the *Gazette* twice."

"No, it's because it's not often I show up in public with such a lovely lady." He paused and adjusted his collar. "Wait, I never show up with a lovely lady."

Maggie smiled and gave a small laugh.

"Have I told you how nice you look tonight?" Jake asked.

"Yes, several times, but don't let that stop you."

It was Jake's turn to smile. "You do look lovely, Maggie.

"You clean up nicely, too."

Jake was as at home in the gray suit as he was in his fireman's turnout coat.

"Did you have fun at the parade today?" he asked. "Every time I saw you, you were rushing off somewhere."

"I was on duty for the auxiliary."

He released a groan. "I never did find out what Bitsy's next project is, and that should worry me."

"More fund-raising."

"That's how I ended up being raffled off to start with."

"This time it's benign. Beautification of Paradise, missions and hospital visitation. No abuse of firemen is planned at this time." Maggie put a hand over her mouth. "Oops, except for the Firemen's Ball this Christmas."

"I knew it. Why doesn't she pick on Sam's department instead of mine?"

"That was discussed at the meeting, but the sheriff's department only has three men."

"That's too bad. No raffling us off, though, right?"

"Oh, no, but it will be a Sadie Hawkins thing, where the girls ask the guys. There are three men for every woman in Paradise."

"Those are some pretty interesting odds." Jake shook his head and eyed the beverage table. "I need a drink. What can I get you? Iced tea?"

"Iced tea would be nice." She smoothed the skirt of her dress, her gaze following Jake as he walked away.

When he'd arrived at her door tonight his eyes had widened after one glance. Of course it was all a matter of timing. Everything had come together nicely. The haircut, the dress. She had Susan to thank for that. Who would have thought two weeks ago that brown-mouse Maggie would come out of her cocoon. If only her parents could see her.

She had to admit, it was fun being all dressed up for one night; as long as Cinderella could go back to her real self in the morning, of course.

Maggie lifted her wrist, fingering the delicate white miniature rosebuds and red satin ribbon. She had Jake to thank for the corsage. Having him escort her had turned out to be much less worrisome than she'd imagined. He'd been on his best behavior and hadn't teased her or anything, which was good because now that she was aware of his tragic past, she was determined not to give him a hard time anymore.

Jake was a handsome man, but more importantly, he was a nice man. A Godly man, who deserved happiness.

All in all, the sort of man any woman would be thrilled to be in the company of. Including her. She enjoyed the growing ease of their burgeoning friendship.

While he could definitely take her breath away, she knew that a man like Jake would never think of her as anything except a friend. That was probably a good thing, Maggie rationalized, since rebuilding her life was taking all her energy at the moment.

Still, her gaze wistfully followed his broad-shouldered silhouette as he disappeared through the crowd, to the far end of the tent. Wouldn't it be nice to have someone like Jake really care for her?

Tonight the past and the future didn't matter, she reminded herself. For a few hours Jake MacLaughlin was hers, and she had one hundred and forty-seven raffle tickets to prove it.

Maggie walked around the room, stopping at a large display on the history of Paradise.

"Oh, Maggie, you look amazing."

She turned and grinned. Her cousin, as usual, was nothing short of regal in a white Grecian sheath. "So do you, Susan. Still a beauty queen."

"Do you like it? I texted a picture to Al. I want him to know what he's missing. Three weeks of fishing with my father is much too long."

"What did Al think of the dress?"

"Oh, you know Al. Not a jealous bone in his body. He sent me back a picture of a bass he caught today."

Maggie laughed.

"Where's your handsome date?" Susan glanced around.

"My escort is getting a beverage."

"Are you glad you came?" Susan asked.

Maggie nodded. "Yes. I really am. Tonight I was forced to realize how small my world had become. Thank you, Susan. For everything."

"That's what fashion-consultant cousins are

for." Susan dispensed an air kiss. "Ooh, look over there. Bernice Harris stopped by as part of her tour. She's doing a photo op for the *Paradise Gazette*."

"The Bison Queen."

"Yes. That's right. Remember I told you about her?"

"I saw her at the parade, signing autographs."

Bernice Harris was hard to miss with a Denver mile-high lacquered blond upsweep and a huge tiara. "What is that hairy thing she's sitting on?"

"That's a stuffed bison. It goes with her on tour to promote the Paradise Valley bison industry."

Maggie shivered. "How unfortunate. That is one ugly bison."

"She'll make up for the ugly bison by getting the local firemen and police hunks in the photo." Susan laughed. "See, there's Duffy now."

"Duffy is so sweet," Maggie commented as he posed with his arm around Bernice. "He bought me an ice-cream cone today at the parade."

"Be very careful of Duffy," Susan said. "He falls in love at least twice a year."

"Oh?"

"Our Duffy is like a big overgrown puppy dog. So unless you're really interested, it's best not to lead him on."

"I hope he doesn't think… Goodness, Susan. Thanks for the heads-up."

"No problem." Susan's eyes widened. "Oh, no, Bernice's dress is caught on the bison. I better go help. Catch up with you later, Mags."

Maggie turned back to the photo gallery of Paradise's historic past. Black-and-white photographs of local citizens and landmarks had been blown up, framed and suspended by wire.

"'Over a hundred and fifty years ago, in 1859, the first settlers came to Paradise. The name started as a joke, but stuck. Paradise was founded during the mining boom and survives thanks to our thriving tourist industry.'"

Maggie whirled around. "Mr. MacLaughlin. You have this memorized?"

"I'm just Mack."

"Mack," she said. The senior MacLaughlin was every bit as handsome as his son tonight, his snow-white hair combed back from a high forehead.

"I've heard the history of this town enough times from my mother over the years that I better have it memorized."

"Has your family always had a hardware store in Paradise?"

"Four generations. The old building was closer to the outskirts of town. Used to be we sat outside the store and knew everyone that passed by name. We can still do that, only not from June to September. Too many tourists."

She smiled.

"Dad, I see you're bending Maggie's ear," Jake said as he approached.

"Just keeping her safe for you, son."

"Almost couldn't find her," he admitted with a smile for Maggie. "Thought for a minute you'd ditched me. Then I remembered you were the girl in the coral dress with the amazing hair."

Speechless, Maggie's face heated at his words.

"Thank you," she said, when he handed her a tall glass.

"So, Dad, are you here alone, or did you bring a date?"

When Jake raised his brows pointedly, Maggie glanced between the two men, trying to read the underlying current.

"I like to enjoy all the ladies in Paradise, son. I'm an equal opportunity flirt. You know that," Mack said with a grin. "Speaking of lovely ladies, here comes Bitsy Harmony."

"Uh-oh," Jake murmured, his warm breath tickling Maggie's ear. "I'll be right back."

"Where are you going?" she asked.

"I'm going to get us a plate of hors d'oeuvres."

"Chicken."

"I'll see if they have any." He grinned.

Bitsy slid into the space Jake vacated. "Where's Jake running off to?"

"Chicken," Mack said.

"I thought as much."

"You look festive tonight, Bitsy," Maggie said. The older woman's hair was wound into a soft braid on the back of her head. She wore a lovely silk shirtdress of royal blue with gold flecks running through the material.

"Thank you. But I tell you, I've been hearing about this mystery woman with Jake from everyone, so I had to check things out for myself."

"Mystery woman?" Maggie asked.

"You. Everyone's abuzz about the beauty on Jake's arm."

Maggie inhaled her tea and began to cough.

"You all right? I know CPR," Bitsy said.

"No. No. Definitely no need." Maggie waved a hand in the air as she cleared her throat. "I'm fine."

"This is always such fun. Have you ever heard such music?" Bitsy continued.

"They're quite good," Maggie agreed.

"Bitsy plays in the Paradise band on occasion," Mack said. "Clarinet." He beamed with pride as his eyes met Bitsy's.

Maggie blinked. The tender expression that passed between the couple was unmistakable. Bitsy Harmony and Mack MacLaughlin were in love.

Her heart melted. Then she froze with the realization that Jake didn't have a clue. Well, she wasn't going to be the one to break the news to him. No way. He obviously had some Bitsy Harmony issues and she was going to keep her distance from that ticking bomb.

The band finished one song and started another. Bitsy looked up at Mack.

"Our song."

Mack paused to listen. "From 1962. Right?"

"What a memory." Bitsy laughed, and Mack joined in at their private joke.

He held out a hand to Bitsy.

"Will you excuse us, Maggie?" he asked.

She smiled. "Of course."

A moment later, Jake appeared at her side and handed her a china plate filled with appetizers. "Where did my dad go?" he said.

"Dancing."

"My dad never dances." Jake craned his neck, his gaze searching the crowded dance floor. "If he's dancing, who's he dancing with?"

Maggie shrugged. "There are so many women here."

Jake took a crab wonton from the plate she held. "Hmm," he said, as he popped it into his mouth.

"Good?" she asked.

"Better than good. Try one?"

"I will. I'm pacing myself."

"Good for you. Someone has to do it. My plan is to eat my way through the evening."

She laughed as he devoured a bacon-wrapped wiener.

"What did Bitsy have to say?" Jake asked as he examined the plate in her hand. He picked up a mini quiche and took a bite.

"Jake, you're going to have to stick around if you expect to keep up."

"Fair enough."

He took the plate from her and placed it on a nearby table.

"I thought we were going to eat those."

"Let's dance," he said, taking her hand.

She trailed behind him. "I don't dance."

Jake stopped and turned around. "Don't or can't?"

"I have many talents, but I can barely walk and chew gum at the same time. I'm a bit clumsy. Realistically, it's safer for the world at large if I do not venture near the dance floor."

"You know, Maggie, that's what I like about you."

"What's that?" she asked, certain he was going to give her a hard time.

"No pretense. I never wonder what's on your mind. You always say what you think."

"I do?" Maggie asked, now curious.

"Well, hello," a sultry female voice interrupted. "You two are certainly having a good time."

Maggie tugged her hand from Jake's and looked over her shoulder to see Sally-Anne approach in a body-clinging black sheath.

"Sally-Anne. You look gorgeous."

"Thank you, Maggie. You, as well."

Maggie ran her fingers through her hair and smiled.

"What do you think, Jake? Like my dress?" Sally-Anne did a twirl for him.

"I am surrounded by beautiful women in beautiful dresses."

Sally-Anne turned to Maggie. "You can tell it's an election year."

Maggie laughed.

"Jake, you owe me a dance from last year," Sally-Anne announced.

"I do?" Jake faltered, his glance moving between the women. "Okay with you, Maggie?"

"Of course." Maggie glanced away, not eager to watch them on the dance floor. Was that a pang of jealousy deep in her heart? Maybe she was hungry; after all, Jake had eaten most of the hors d'oeuvres he brought back, all by himself.

She weaved through people, targeting the buffet table, and had almost reached the casseroles when Beck Hollander stepped into her path.

"Hi, Maggie," he said as he adjusted his glasses. "You, uh, you look good."

"Thank you, Beck." She assessed his neatly pressed black shirt and the black jeans and white skinny tie. Even his disheveled hair had a semblance of order tonight. The most remarkable change was the missing earbuds and smartphone. "You look very dapper."

"Dapper?" The tips of Beck's ears beamed a heated red. "Is that good?"

"Yes! Look it up."

"Do you…do you want to dance?'

"Oh, Beck, thank you. I really don't dance. But I'd be happy to discuss quantum physics with you later if the party slows down."

Beck grinned.

"You have a nice smile. Smile more often."

Directly across the room, the redheaded teen from the café waved at them.

"There's Julia," Maggie said.

"Yeah."

"She likes you, Beck."

The teen shook his head.

"Is that a problem?"

"Liberal arts," he mumbled.

"Excuse me?"

"Colorado State. Liberal arts major."

Maggie inhaled sharply. "Beck Hollander, are you telling me that you're an academic snob?"

Beck squirmed uncomfortably.

"I'm appalled."

"Okay, fine. I'll talk to her." Head bowed, he

shoved his hands into his pockets and dragged his sneakered feet toward Julia.

Pleased with her minor matchmaking success, Maggie strolled to where her aunt stood supervising the dessert buffet.

"Margaret, aren't you enchanting?" She came around the table and held Maggie's hands while she inspected her outfit from head to toe. "I've heard all about that dress."

"Enchanting?" Maggie rolled it on her tongue. "I like that word."

"In my day they said *fetching*, but that sounds like a dog term."

"You're right, Aunt B. *Enchanting* sounds like a princess cartoon. It makes me feel like twirling around and breaking into song."

"Oh, Maggie, you're such a treat. Do you know that?"

"I feel liberated, Aunt B. Free to be whatever I desire."

"Ah, so that's it. Instead of your wedding day, this is your independence day."

"Yes. Exactly." Maggie couldn't help but grin widely.

"May I congratulate you on the teaching position?"

Maggie gasped. "What? I got the job? Who told you?"

"I made a lunch delivery from the café to the school-board offices Friday afternoon."

"Does everyone know?"

"No." Her aunt laughed. "I ran into Beck's father. He told me. He's pretty close-lipped and I like to think I'm not as indiscreet as others in this town."

"Let's not tell anyone yet. Please. At least not until I have the official word."

"Our secret." Aunt Betty nodded with a gestured zip to her lips. "Now you can tell me where the handsome fire chief is."

"Sally-Anne caught him for a dance."

Aunt B cocked her head. "Ah, but the music has stopped and Sally-Anne is not a 'catch and release' kind of gal. Go reel him back in before Sally-Anne thinks he doesn't have a home."

"Oh, he'll find me. I'm not worried," Maggie said with a newfound confidence. She examined the dessert table. "Is that your German torte?"

"It is. Hazelnut. Not Bitsy's pie, though I do have a modest following of torte-heads here in Paradise."

"Torte-heads?"

As Maggie laughed with her aunt, the warmth of Jake's hand touched her waist. A shiver raced up her arms.

"Are you going to save some of your torte for me, Mrs. Jones?" he asked.

"There you are, Jake. Of course I will. First you had better take my niece to dinner before there isn't anything left. I see the mayor is preparing to test the microphones."

"Uh-oh." He looked to Maggie as he led her toward the main buffet table. "Why didn't you help me back there with Sally-Anne?"

"Help you? Oh, no, no, no. That isn't in my job description. I won the escort, not the drama."

Jake watched her, seemingly considering her words.

"Besides," she concluded, "if you're going to be the most eligible bachelor in Paradise you're going to have to suffer the consequences."

"Good answer." He shook his head and smiled, appeased. "Are you ready for some real food? We ought to fortify ourselves before the mayor and the town council get on stage for their annual 'state of Paradise' address."

She looped her arm through his. "I'm starving. Let's go."

The moonlit sky illuminated the front porch as they approached the door of the little cottage. Jake walked beside Maggie, and she found her steps slowing to delay the end of the evening.

"The house looks good. Cozy," he said, observing the potted plants in front of them.

Overhead, a wind chime sang a gentle melody in the slight breeze.

"Thanks."

"How'd the interview go?" he asked as he allowed her up the steps first.

"My aunt says I got the job."

"What?"

She glanced over her shoulder.

He stood with his foot on the bottom step and looked at her. "Have you accepted?"

"I haven't gotten official notification yet. But yes, I'm going to accept."

He nodded thoughtfully, walked up the steps and held the screen. Maggie pulled her keys from her bag and unlocked the front door, her mind tumbling with thoughts.

What did that nod mean in guy-speak? Was he glad she was staying?

"Do you want to come in for a cup of tea?"

"Sure."

She touched a wall switch, bringing the small living room to life. The dining room table, covered with newspaper, had parts and tools scattered on it again.

"Latest project?"

"Yes. I'm working on a decorative, outdoor wind chime using leftover bicycle parts."

"Bicycle parts. Hmm. Ever thought about marketing your ideas?"

"Oh, maybe. Someday."

He glanced around, sniffing the air. "You smell something?"

"I burned popcorn last night," she admitted.

"Not sure that's it, unless you melted the entire microwave."

"No, only the popcorn and the fire alarm did go off."

"Glad to hear that. You reset it, correct?"

"Yes, Chief."

Maggie kicked off her new heels and put on a kettle of water. "Tonight was fun. I didn't expect that."

"In truth, neither did I," he said.

She plopped into a kitchen chair and flexed her sore feet. "Now I know why they only do it once a year."

"Feels good to have my yearly bath taken care of," Jake replied with a yawn.

She laughed. "Somehow I suspect you're always squeaky clean."

"Is that so bad?"

"Not at all, so long as you're willing to play in the dirt on occasion."

He smiled at the reference, a twinkle in the amber depths of his eyes.

"It was fun to watch the young and the old in Paradise all coming together," Maggie said.

"The kids will be gone soon. Everyone leaves Paradise," Jake mused as he loosened his tie.

"Do you think so? I think they'll come back. Doesn't everyone come back eventually?"

"Maybe. You and I both did."

She stood and pulled clean mugs out of the

dishwasher. "I was only a summer guest in Paradise. I can't tell you how much I looked forward to coming back each year to vacation Bible school and outings on Paradise Lake and riding my bike."

"No bicycle in Denver?"

"No. Busy streets and my parents were busy people."

"That's too bad. Every kid should have the chance to ride their bike from dawn to dusk."

"I agree. What did you do after you left Paradise, Jake? What brought you back?"

"College, marriage, Denver Fire Department."

"Married young?"

"Yeah." He fiddled with the empty mug she'd placed in front of him. "Seems like no one does that anymore. Diana, my wife, all she ever wanted was to do the whole domestic thing. Babies and all. We put that last bit on hold while we finished college." He paused. "Then we both worked to pay off student loans. Not an extra penny between us. Life was simple. I think it was true that we were too young and naive to know we weren't supposed to live on love."

His gaze me hers. "Crazy, huh?"

"Not crazy," Maggie said. "Marriages used to last. Maybe we were both raised to believe you stuck it out when things got tough, you didn't run. Quitting simply was not an option. Which is why I ran before the marriage."

"There's a lot to be said for timing," Jake said.

"Agreed." She put a basket of teas on the table. "My parents married later in life, but Aunt Betty and Uncle Bob married young. They're going on forty years."

"That's amazing in today's world."

"How did you lose her, Jake?" Maggie released the words gently, knowing the question had to be asked. She was tired of hearing everything about Jake from unexpected and secondhand sources.

He took a deep breath. "Head-on collision. Drunk driver. I was on the scene. First responder. The vehicle exploded." His head dropped as he spoke, his eyes closed, as if pushing away the memories "Couldn't...couldn't save her."

"Oh, no..." Maggie's breath stuck in her lungs and her eyes filled with moisture. Instinctively, she reached out to touch his hand. He enfolded her fingers in his palm and stared unseeing at the sight of their hands together.

They were both quiet for moments.

"I wouldn't have made it without my faith." Jake shook his head. "I was ugly and miserable, blaming myself. Yet every time I called on Him, He was there for me."

Maggie stared at Jake. "Why would you blame yourself?"

"I should have been able to save her. That's my job."

"You can't protect everyone."

"My brain knows that but my heart has never believed the words were true."

"What does God say?"

He gave a wry smile. "We circle around the topic."

"How long has it been?" she asked.

"Ten years."

"That's a long time to be alone."

He sat back in the chair and yanked off his tie and placed it on the table.

The whistling kettle hissed and called to Maggie. She reached for a potholder and poured hot water into the mugs, then returned the kettle to the stove and sat down again.

"You know this is the first time I've actually been out with a woman since I lost her."

She arched a brow. "I'm honored."

"I guess Bitsy's crazy fireman raffle wasn't such a bad idea after all."

"I wasn't too thrilled at first myself."

"I got that part right away." He laughed.

"The entire evening was fun. Memorable," she said.

"Yeah?"

"Uh-huh."

"What part did you like best?'

"When you picked me up and looked at me like I was beautiful."

He paused, as if taken aback by her response. "You are beautiful."

She shrugged.

"You know, we actually have a lot in common," Jake mused. "We both returned to Paradise for the same reason. To hide. The people of Paradise took me into their hearts. The love I found in this town has erased most of the pain and allowed me to start over. I think you're going to find the same thing."

He took a deep breath and tore open the packet of tea, pulling out the bag. Slowly he dipped it into his mug. "What I'm trying to say is I take one day at a time. That was my vow when I moved here. I don't look down the road. Don't worry about tomorrow."

"That's your plan, huh? I'm not sure I'm there yet. I'm still worrying about six months down the road, myself," she said.

Jake grinned. "I'm glad we've become friends, Maggie. I like being with you. I don't want to stop. And I don't want to think any further than today. Is that okay?"

"Sure. I'll think about tomorrow and you think about today. That can be our plan."

He stared into her eyes for several moments, before slowly leaning forward. His breath touched her face as he paused to silently ask permission.

"Yes," she whispered.

Maggie closed her eyes in time to feel his lips barely graze hers. She swallowed a sigh and opened her eyes.

"Okay?" he questioned, his expression solemn.

Her heart continued to bump wildly against her chest, even as she nodded and pretended a peace she was far from feeling.

"Maggie?"

She raised her head. "Yes."

"I really do smell something burning."

Maggie frowned. "Jake, nothing is burning."

"Yet, my nose disagrees." He slid back his chair. "Mind if I look around?"

"Have at it," she said.

"What's in here?" He pulled open a door.

"Hot water tank."

Jake pulled a small flashlight from his pocket and inspected the tank. "Looks okay. No leaking. Keep the area around it free from dust."

"Yes, sir."

Maggie followed him as he moved down the hall to the bathroom. "Gas wall heater. These things are dangerous."

"Jake, it's summer. I've never used the thing and it's about forty years old. I would never use it. Trust me to have some common sense."

At least he had the wisdom not to remind her of past indiscretions.

He pointed to the last door. "Bedroom?"

She nodded.

"May I?"

Maggie groaned. The room was an impressive mess, with clothes tossed on every surface.

A quilt had been haphazardly thrown over the mismatched sheets and the pillows were falling off the bed.

"I was in a rush." Her face flamed. "I got so busy soldering the wind chimes that I lost track of time."

"Soldering?" His eyes rounded.

Maggie released a small gasp. "I left the soldering gun on."

She raced down the hall, her dress fluttering around her. The hot metal odor only intensified as they approached the living room.

Jake's cheek twitched with the obvious effort of saying nothing while Maggie unplugged the tool.

"I'm sorry. I'm sorry. It wasn't touching anything." She winced. "I'm really sorry. Sometimes I just get caught up in what I'm doing."

"I'd tell you that I understand. But I don't. There's something about you that seems to attract trouble and I'd like that to stop."

Maggie gave a slow and thoughtful nod.

He met her gaze. "Maggie," he said, his voice low and dangerously calm, "I'm your friend. I care about you. I don't think I could handle it if something happened to you and I could have prevented it."

He released a breath and shuddered. "Not again. Not in this lifetime."

Chapter Eight

"Margaret, when are you coming home?" Her father's voice rang out clearly as he put her on speakerphone.

"Good morning, Dad. I was calling to wish you a happy Father's Day."

"I'll be happy when you come home. Besides, Father's Day was yesterday."

"I called yesterday and got voice mail."

"We were at a new program at the museum. You know we're never available on the weekends."

"Right."

"When did you say you were coming home, Margaret?" her father asked again.

"I'm not coming home."

"Excuse me?"

"I'm about to accept a temporary teaching position in Paradise. This is my home now."

Her mother spoke up. "I didn't realize there was a university in Paradise."

Maggie cleared her throat. "High school. I'm teaching at a high school."

"Teaching what?" her mother asked.

"Junior and senior level science. Mostly chemistry, physics and some botany and biology."

Her mother gasped. "You can't be serious. What about your PhD? The ink is barely dry on your diploma. Then there's your student-loan repayment. You didn't spend all that time and money on your doctorate to teach a bunch of teenagers how to dissect a frog."

"You're exaggerating, Mother."

"Am I?"

"At any rate. This is what I'm doing until May. I'm taking a break from college academia. I've been going to school since I was five years old. I'm tired of being a professional student."

"Are you tired of the fact that you're on the tenure track at thirty-two? Thanks to us, I might add."

"I do thank you, Mother. Both of you. For everything." She took a deep breath. "Now it's time for me to live my own life."

"Interesting phraseology. What exactly does that mean, Margaret?"

"It means I get to choose from now on."

"Choose what?" her father asked.

"Choose everything, Dad."

"Be sensible, Margaret. You're going to give up

the dreams you've worked so hard for, for what? What exactly does Paradise have to offer you?"

"Your dreams, Dad. Yours and Mom's. As for me, well, I'm not sure yet. The only thing I know for certain is that I need time to think, so I can decide exactly what I want to do with the rest of my life."

"What if you fail?"

"In this situation, failure is an option. It's my life. In my heart, I feel as though, well, like the Lord is calling me to take a step out in faith, toward the life He has for me."

"Oh, you're not going to start with that God stuff again, are you?" her mother groaned. "Ronald, this is your brother's fault. I knew sending her to that place in the summers was a bad idea."

"Mother, I've been a Christian for years. You know that."

"I thought it was a phase that you would outgrow."

"How do you outgrow God?"

"I will not discuss this any further," her mother returned.

Maggie could visualize her mother's expression of distain with clarity.

"That's fine. It wasn't my intention to make you uncomfortable."

Her mother cleared her throat. "Have you spoken to your fiancé?"

"Ex-fiancé. I spoke to him before I left. When I personally returned his ring."

"I'm sure he's devastated."

"Yes. He is. Now he has to find another mentor for tenureship. I was never the object of his affection, Mother. He was desperately in love with our family's academic status."

"That isn't true, Margaret."

"It is true, and it's really a moot point now."

"Will you be coming to get your things?" her father asked. "We've decided to turn your room into an office for your mother."

"Sure. Yes. Let me schedule a moving truck. Will this Saturday work for you?"

"Yes. Very good."

"Did I say happy Father's Day?" Maggie asked.

"You did. Have a good day, Margaret, and remember that we can't hold your position at the college for much longer."

"I understand that, Dad. Goodbye. I love you."

"Goodbye."

Maggie set down her cell and realized her other hand was closed into a tense fist, her short nails digging into her palm.

Warm and fuzzy, her parents were not. They cared in their own way, which unfortunately generally consisted mostly of reading between the lines. With a microscope. Aunt Betty was right, her father and Uncle Bob were as different as two brothers could be.

What would have happened if she'd actually grown up in Paradise instead of simply spending summers here?

Maybe she'd be more like Susan and less like the coward she'd become.

Guilt gnawed at her as she paced the kitchen, mulling over the conversation with her parents. How was it they always managed to make her feel like a failure?

Am I missing it here, Lord? No, she didn't think so. She was determined to look forward and not back and things were looking very good. Why, she had a lovely little house, and a newly planted garden. A new job, too.

Maggie glanced at the clock. Too early for work. Unless she walked to work and then stopped by Patti Jo's and treated herself to something special to celebrate her new life in Paradise.

She wasn't going to allow her parents to steal her joy. Locking the door, she headed down the street, with a smile on her face.

"Hi, Mack," Maggie called out as she approached his house.

Mack pulled his head from beneath the hood of a vintage Mustang.

"Mornin', Maggie. Where's your bike? Do you need a ride to work?"

"No, thanks, it's a lovely day. I prefer to walk."

She stopped at the bottom of his driveway. "What are you doing?"

He stood straight and wiped his hands on a greasy rag. "I'm trying to get this baby fixed for Bitsy. That tank she drives is on its last legs."

"Need any help? I'm pretty good with engines."

"Why am I not surprised? I might take you up on that offer later."

"You do that. Just holler."

"I will." Mack paused and opened his mouth, and then closed it as though he suddenly thought better of it.

"Was there something else?"

"Uh, no. I guess not."

"Have a great day," she said.

Maggie continued along the residential street until she reached Main. She took a shortcut through the alley to Patti Jo's Café and Bakery, where she pulled open the familiar red door.

"One tall black coffee and a chocolate scone, please, Julia." She dug in her wallet for exact change.

"Here you go," Julia said. The teen looked at Maggie with a question on her face.

Maggie frowned, perplexed. "Everything okay, Julia?"

Julia nodded. At the same time two customers slowly walked by and stared at Maggie.

Something was definitely going on and eventually she'd figure it out. After all, this was Paradise, and there were no secrets here.

She left the café and stepped outside, turning her face to the sunshine as she walked down the street. Today she'd only think about pleasant things, like the new outfit that she was wearing, a white eyelet-trimmed, peach peasant blouse with green capris.

Or maybe she'd think about Jake and his feather-soft kiss instead. Her heart needed no encouragement to change the subject of her thoughts. Of course, it was a once-in-a-lifetime kiss, not to be repeated, which meant she'd savor it even more.

Turning the corner, she halted, her coffee sloshing forward through the sip hole. A long line had formed outside the fix-it shop. A line that consisted wholly of men. Men of various shapes, sizes and ages stood with appliances and equipment in hand. What was going on? Were they having a sale and no one told her?

She stepped carefully toward the shop. Several heads turned and elbows jostled each other as the customers turned to look at her. Yes. They were all men. What was going on?

"Hi, Maggie!"

"Hello?" she said with a wary smile. Did she know the man? Maybe from the Founder's Day supper?

Faces ranging from familiar to not so familiar greeted her with eager smiles.

Standing at the head of the line was Duffy McKenna, holding a large cardboard box. She didn't want to know what was inside that box.

His freckled face lit up when he saw her. "Good morning, Maggie."

"Duffy?"

"You look lovely today," he said.

"Ah, thank you. You are aware that we don't open for another thirty minutes, right?"

"That's okay, I'll wait. I've been here for two hours. Can't give up my spot."

"Two hours? That must be important stuff in that box." She shook her head. "I'll see what I can do about opening a little early this morning."

"Thanks, Maggie." Duffy grinned and elbowed the elderly man next to him in line.

Maggie knocked on the door of the shop and Beck peeked out from behind the blinds. She heard a click and the door finally swung open. She slipped inside and shut it firmly behind her.

"What's going on?" she asked, unable to keep the panic from her voice.

He shrugged.

"No. Seriously, Beck. This is not the time for monosyllabic. *What is going on?*"

"I think you have a few admirers."

"You think all of those men are here for me?"

"Uh-huh."

"Why. How?"

"Some rumor."

Maggie put her coffee and scone on the counter. "Now what? I'm not in the paper again, am I?" She released a short, nervous laugh.

Beck nodded.

"I'm in the paper again?" Maggie's gaze searched the room until she found the paper near the cash register.

"Front page."

She skimmed the article about the Founder's Day event, and then unfolded the paper. Then her mouth dropped open. A photo of her watching the band with the caption: "Maggie Jones, who's arrived in Paradise to find a husband, enjoys the Founder's Day supper. More photos on page four."

Rustling the paper, she turned the pages quickly to page four. "I'm only on the front page. That's a plus."

Except the damage was already done. And this certainly explained her strange morning. Once again, panic welled up inside. She waved a hand toward the street. "What am I going to do?"

As if on cue, a loud knock rattled the door.

"We don't open for thirty minutes," Maggie called.

"It's Bitsy Harmony."

Maggie unlocked the door and yanked it open. "You have a fix-it emergency?" she asked.

"Oh, I'm not here for that. I want to know what your strategy is to deal with this." Bitsy slapped the newspaper in her hand against her palm. "And that." She nodded toward the ever growing line.

Maggie closed the door. "Strategy? Are you kidding me? I still don't have a clue how this happened, much less how to stop it."

"You sell papers."

"I what?"

"The last two issues that featured you on the front page broke all records. The newspaper is a dying form of communication. Can't blame the *Paradise Gazette* for trying to stir up revenue."

"I can't? I was planning to discuss the word *slander* with them." Maggie shook her head. "I should demand a retraction. Yes. That's it. A front page apology, as well."

"That'll only irritate folks. You're new to town. You can't afford that kind of alienation. A new teacher and all."

"How did you know…" She closed her eyes for a moment and then opened them. "Never mind." Maggie sagged against the counter. "I can't just do *nothing*. Did you see that line out there?"

"Paradise has always had an inordinately large population of men, compared to the number of available women," Bitsy mused.

"That's not my fault."

"I recommend that you let them think your affections lie elsewhere," Bitsy remarked.

Maggie blinked. "What do you mean?"

"You like Jake."

"You like the chief?" Beck asked, breaking into the conversation.

Maggie inhaled sharply as she turned to the teenager, just realizing he was still in the room. "We're friends. The chief and I are friends."

Bitsy looked at Beck. "Would you excuse us for a few minutes?"

Beck dragged himself slowly to the back of the shop.

"That young man has a crush on you," Bitsy said quietly.

"Beck?" Maggie glanced at the door that had closed behind him.

"Yup. Be careful. He's impressionable, and I'd say he's jealous of the chief."

"I'll be careful, but you're the one who mentioned Jake."

"So I did. For good reason. There's not a thing wrong with allowing folks to make assumptions. They're going to make them anyhow. After all, this is Paradise. So why not lead them in another direction."

Maggie put a hand to her head, and then realized her ponytail was gone. "You want them to think…Jake and I?"

Bitsy nodded.

"Oh, I'm not sure that's a good idea. In fact what you're suggesting is exactly what Aunt Betty calls diving straight from the frying pan into the fire."

"There's a difference when it's by choice. Then it's called long range planning."

"That makes sense, I think."

"Of course it does. You're simply going to take what looks like a problem and turn it around to benefit your goals here in Paradise."

Obviously Bitsy had confidence that Maggie actually had goals. Maggie glanced at the wall clock. The minute hand joined the hour hand. Quarter to nine. Time to open the shop. She swallowed and reached for the door.

She knew the moment Jake entered the shop. How was it she had extra sensory perception when the man was around?

"Please don't tell me you have a broken toaster. I've spent the better part of my morning looking at toasters. Most of them suffering from user error."

He chuckled. "Good to see you, too, Maggie."

She wiped her chin with an oil rag and fought to ignore him, though her traitorous eyes continued to sneak glances at his profile.

"Actually, I'm here in an official capacity."

"Of course you are," she mumbled. Apparently he hadn't spent restless hours thinking about their kiss. No, the man was all business on a Monday morning.

"The sheriff called me. He's had a few complaints that your customers were parking in the fire lane."

"You handle traffic, too?"

"I'm the fire marshal."

Silence stretched.

"Earth to Maggie?"

"Hmm?" She reached for a Phillips screwdriver. Jake's hand covered hers.

Maggie jerked back at the contact and met his gaze.

With a small frown, Jake reached out and held her chin.

"What are you doing?" Maggie asked, as she attempted to pull away.

"Hold still. There's grease on your chin." He took the rag from her hand and gently wiped her chin before releasing her.

"Thank you." Face ablaze, Maggie turned away.

"What's going on in that computer-processing head of yours?"

"I'm appalled and humiliated that there was a line of men outside the shop this morning."

"Ah, the picture in the *Gazette*. That explains why you're hiding behind that ball cap and those baggy coveralls."

She picked up the patch of oil-stained rag from

the counter. "I'm not hiding. I didn't want to get my clothes dirty, so I changed when I got to work."

"Right." He cleared his throat. "What happened?"

"Ralph Meyer—the butcher—brought me bacon. Not ordinary bacon, either. It's specially cured with a tad bit of maple syrup and honey." She sighed. "Andy Pickering, the librarian, gave me flowers from his garden." She met Jake's gaze. "And Duffy. Duffy was at the head of the line. He brought in a laptop. In about one hundred pieces."

"I'll take care of Duffy, but there's nothing I can do about the rest of them."

"I'd like to know who wrote that article. Who thinks I'm looking for a husband?"

"Are you?"

Maggie jerked back. "No. I only just got rid of…" She stopped when she realized Jake was grinning.

"I'm glad you find this so amusing."

"Not amusing. More like eye-opening. Seeing you all worked up, that is."

She took a deep calming breath. "What can I do for you, Fire Marshal MacLaughlin?"

"I came to ask you to remind your customers that parking along Main Street is only for thirty minutes and never in the fire lane. Ever."

"You want me to police the streets of Paradise?"

"A friendly reminder when they come in. That's all."

"I'll see what I can do," Maggie said as she tossed the rag in her hand down.

"You do that."

Maggie gritted her teeth at the laughter that underlined his words.

"Look, I've had a really bad morning, *Chief.* To top it off, I spoke with my parents earlier. They felt the need to reiterate their platform, which is, of course, that I should move back home like a good little girl." She slapped the counter with her open palm. "I won't do it."

"Whoa. You're full of surprises, Maggie."

"Am I?" She frowned. "Not really—normally I'm as uncomplicated as vanilla ice cream."

"I like vanilla ice cream." He leaned closer to the counter and waggled his eyebrows. "Quite a bit as it happens."

She pointed to the door. "Stand in line."

"You're not good for a man's ego." He glanced over at the duffel bag and sneakers in the corner. "Those your running shoes?"

"Yes. Sometimes I go running after work."

"Really? Care to go for a jog with me sometime?"

"You run?"

"Yeah. What do you say?"

"Maybe." She gave a noncommittal shrug as she rested her arms on the counter. She couldn't think. Her mind was swirling in a thousand directions at one time.

"How about this Sunday, after church?"

"I don't know."

"Maggie, I'm not asking you to marry me. It's two friends getting together to enjoy the great outdoors."

Two friends.

Was that all they were?

Then she remembered her conversation with Bitsy. Maggie shot straight up and slapped her forehead.

"Are you okay?" Jake asked.

"I almost forgot."

"Forgot what?"

Here she was discouraging Jake, when Bitsy wanted her to encourage him. She swallowed, gathering courage. The important thing was to not mention Bitsy. Jake had a knee-jerk reaction when Bitsy's name was mentioned.

"Maggie, are you in there?"

"Yes. Yes." She mustered up a smile. "Maybe you could help me."

"You're smiling. What's up?"

"My life is spinning out of control and I really want things to settle down. I'd like to go back to flying under the radar and living my life without complication."

"And that involves me…how?"

"You said we're friends, right?"

"Ye-e-ss." He said the word slowly, almost as if he realized that they were about to step into dangerous territory.

"You do things alone and I do things alone."

He narrowed his eyes.

"Maybe we could do some things together. Friends and all."

His head jerked back a tad at the unexpected words. "But you just said… Wait a minute. Are you asking me out?"

"No," Maggie huffed. "Oh, never mind." She waved a dismissive hand through the air. "I knew this was a ridiculous idea."

"Hang on there. No need to get all worked up. Give it to me one more time. I'm a little slow today. Chuck had an emergency last night."

"Is Chuck okay?"

"Yeah. Turns out he managed to pull the laces off my boots and swallow them." Jake winced. "Everything came out all right eventually, according to the vet."

"Glad to hear that." Maggie grimaced. "I think."

"So run that by me again," he said.

"I'm asking you to be my escort around town. Join me for dinner and such."

"I didn't know you could cook."

"That was a hypothetical example. I can do carryout, you know."

"Right. And toaster pastries." He shook his head. "What's going on, Maggie?"

"I need my life to return to normal."

"Define normal."

"I want that line outside to go away. I want people to say 'Maggie who?' when my name comes up in conversation."

"This is Paradise. Good luck."

Jake crossed his arms and stared thoughtfully at her. "However, we are friends and I am willing to give your plan a shot if you think it will be good for your mental health. Because when you're distracted trouble always follows."

A delicious shiver raced over Maggie as he stared at her; then reality slapped her in the face.

Jake MacLaughlin was now on Team Maggie. She'd be spending more time with the man who ignited crazy sparks of unfamiliar emotions inside her. She took off her glasses and rubbed the throbbing place in the middle of her forehead.

Two friends helping each other out. That's what she told him. Now all she had to do was convince her heart that's all they were.

Jake washed his hands in the sink before reaching for the truck keys. His stomach growled and the thought of a nice thick steak made him quicken his pace in anticipation. Monday meant the surf-and-turf special at the Prospector.

He was out the door and unlocking his truck when he remembered his conversation with Maggie this morning and her crazy idea about hanging out together to quash her suitor problem.

Thinking about Maggie went deeper than her goofy plan. Maybe even deeper than that kiss on Saturday, though he'd given that some thought, too. It had been a chaste kiss, as far as kisses went. Still, once his lips touched hers and he'd tasted the softness, the sweetness, the goodness that was Maggie, he realized he was in trouble.

They'd avoided discussing the kiss, but eventually it would come up again, because he couldn't help but want more even with the sirens and warning lights blazing all around the woman.

Yet, with Maggie it was more than the possibility of kisses. He enjoyed her smiles and the way her eyes lit up when she laughed. Enjoyed their conversations. She was one smart woman and kept him on his toes. Made him forget that he was nearly eight years older than her.

He wracked his mind trying to think of a legitimate excuse for dropping by the little house. Should he call? No, that would sound premeditated. Though she was the one who said they should do their alone stuff together. Dinner more than counted, right?

"I was in the neighborhood."

He practiced the line several times before rejecting it as lame.

Okay, he'd head over there and hope he thought of something really clever before he arrived.

When he pulled the truck to a stop in front of the cottage, he spotted her sitting on the front porch. "Hi," he said, strolling up the drive.

She looked up from the stack of papers in her hands and smiled.

Definitely a welcoming smile. He'd take that as a good omen.

"I thought we were going running on Sunday?"

"We are, but I was hungry for a steak. Can you take a break from your work if I promise you the best steak this side of the Rockies?"

She glanced at the paperwork and set it aside. "Your offer sounds better than an evening of paperwork."

"Great. I'm thinking the Prospector restaurant in town. They have twice-baked potatoes the size of melons. Oh, and the salads. Fresh and crisp, with their secret ingredient—the house dressing."

"Stop," Maggie demanded. "You're torturing me."

Jake grinned. "Good. So you're on board?"

"Like this?" She glanced down at her jeans and blouse.

"Overdressed. This is a down-home place. Just a bunch of Colorado cowboys."

"Let me grab my hat and saddle up my horse."

Jake laughed. And kept laughing, all the way to the restaurant. Maggie kept the conversation going throughout the meal, as well.

"Did you have enough to eat?" he asked when she slid her plate aside.

"Yes. I'm stuffed. Thank you."

"That was local beef and local fish."

"Delicious."

"Ever do any fishing?"

"Fish? Sure, summers with my uncle."

Jake nodded and raised a brow. "Live bait?"

"Of course." Maggie smiled triumphantly.

"Bait your own line?"

"Do I look like a sissy to you?" She wiped her mouth with her napkin and leveled a haughty look at him.

"No, ma'am. No sissies here."

The waitress cleared their table and took an order for the dessert of the day. Peach cobbler.

"I will forever think of Bitsy Harmony when I hear the word *peach*."

"That's too bad," Jake said, frowning.

"How long has Bitsy lived in Paradise?"

"She's a newcomer, only been here thirty-five years or so."

"Thirty-five years?" Maggie sputtered.

"According to Mack, she came to Paradise to

take care of her grandmother. Bitsy was a friend of my mother's, too."

"Oh? Was Bitsy ever married?"

"I have no idea."

"Don't you ask?"

Jake shuddered. "Are you kidding? Why would I do that? I don't want to know any more about Bitsy than I absolutely have to."

"Oh, that's hilarious, Jake. You've known the woman all your life and you have no idea if she is single, married or divorced?"

"Yeah, and that's the way I like it. Our paths cross a lot professionally, but Bitsy and I don't need to know any more about each other's lives than what's necessary to get our jobs done."

"Why is it you dislike her so much?"

"I don't dislike her. I'm just bothered by her. Regularly."

Maggie folded her hands on the table. "Bothered is sort of vague."

"I'm a private man, and the woman hasn't figured out that she needs to keep her business out of mine."

He lowered his voice. "One thing you need to know about Bitsy is the more information you share with her, the more she figures she's got carte blanche to meddle in your life."

"Still, aren't you a teeny bit curious about her?"

"I didn't say I don't know stuff. What I said

is I don't need to know. There's a difference."

Jake shook his head and took a long swig of his iced tea.

"I see. I'm learning there are a lot of characters in this town, and life in Paradise is certainly not boring," Maggie said after the waitress served dessert and coffee.

"Never that." He pulled a piece of warm crust off his cobbler and popped it in his mouth.

Maggie looked around the restaurant. "This place is busy. I guess that's good for me."

"I don't follow."

"The Paradise grapevine," she said.

It took Jake a moment to process her words. Once he did a heavy cloud of disappointment hovered over him. "Oh, your little plan."

"This will help the situation. Don't you think?"

"Yes. I do." Jake reached out and covered her small hands with his.

Maggie startled in her chair, her gaze meeting his.

"Enhancing the scene," he said.

She carefully slipped her hands from beneath his. "You're quite the actor, but I need my hands to eat."

"Right."

An awkward silence stretched between them.

"You know what you need?" Jake asked.

"What's that?" Maggie asked. Her eyes were curious as she waited for his response.

"A dog."

"Wow. That was totally random."

"Passing thought."

"You should have let it pass right on by, because I'm really not a dog person."

"Then what about a cat?" he asked.

"No cats."

"No dogs. No cats. I'm guessing you think you're not a people person, either, and yet, everyone loves you."

She looked taken aback. "How do you know that's what I think?"

"Oh, I'm a little more intuitive than you've pegged me for. I may be the fire chief in a town the size of a postage stamp, but I get around."

Maggie laughed. "Seriously? That's your defense. You are possibly one of the smartest and shrewdest men I have ever known."

The waitress interrupted to refill their coffee cups.

"Besides," Maggie added, tapping a finger on the table, "my landlord might balk at the idea of a dog or a cat."

Jake waved a hand. "You've got an inside with the landlord."

"I don't know. Owning an animal sounds like a huge commitment."

Jake smiled slowly. Yeah, that's exactly what it sounded like to him.

"Why the random pitch?" she asked.

"Animals are good protection."

"Ah, so this is about my little accidents."

He shrugged. "I'm thinking about your safety. Maybe you should, too."

Maggie sighed and picked up her mug. She sipped her coffee and stared past him, absorbed in thought.

"How long is your contract with the high school?" he asked.

"Basically, one school year. That will carry me through May. The teacher I'm replacing is having…"

"Triplets. First triplets in Paradise. Talk of the town until you arrived and stole the limelight."

"I didn't… Well, never mind. What I'm getting at is that she's utilizing the Family Leave and Medical Act to take an extended leave."

"Family is important."

Maggie nodded.

"You plan to have kids someday?" he asked.

"Yes, but I thought growing up and having a life of my own should come first, though."

He scooped up a forkful of cobbler. "Good plan in theory."

"What's that mean?"

"It means that sometimes the Lord hands you a different road map."

"That's true."

"Paradise is beautiful in the winter," he said.

"You're just full of random observations tonight."

"I guess. Ever ice-skate? There's a pond outside of town. Of course, we give it a little help."

"I never had the chance to skate. Do you?"

"All my life. We like a friendly hockey game around here. Beat the pants off those young kids every time."

Maggie grinned.

"And you should see how they light up the park in the town square for Christmas."

"I imagine it's a scene out of Currier and Ives," she said on a wistful note. With a finger she traced circles through the condensation on her water glass.

"When they can't find a willing stand-in to play Santa, Mack does it."

Maggie gave a wry smile, obviously picturing Mack in a red suit.

"So you're here for a year. Then what?" He knew he was rambling, but seemed unable to stop himself. Despite his desire to not look down the road, Jake felt an obstinate urgency to know exactly what path Maggie's future would take her down.

"I honestly don't know."

"Couldn't you 'not know' right here in Paradise?"

She smiled and cut a piece of cobbler with her

fork. "Pretty good cobbler, isn't it? Not as good as Bitsy's pie, but pretty good."

"Nice try," he said, referring to her segue.

Maggie arched a brow, and then winked. "A little trick I learned from dealing with my parents."

He nodded and took a bite of his dessert, chewing thoughtfully. When he set down his fork, he looked her in the eye. "Just so you know, that trick won't work with me."

"I was afraid of that."

Chapter Nine

"Morning, Maggie."

She jumped and turned around, nearly dropping her bike. Jake appeared from around the corner. He wore a ball cap high on the back of his head. When he smiled at her, her heart did a funny little dance.

"Jake, what are you doing here? It's only six o'clock in the morning."

"I got a message I was supposed to meet you at the hardware store at six sharp." He glanced at his watch. "Right on time."

"I didn't leave you a message. I would never be so presumptuous with your time. Especially on a Saturday."

"Where are we going anyhow?" Jake asked.

"*I'm* driving to Denver to get my stuff." She paced on the cement parking lot. "I don't understand. Your father rented me the truck yesterday and I told him I'd pick it up this morning."

"Oh, that explains a lot, since he's the one who left me the message." Jake removed his cap and slapped it back on. "Driving by yourself?"

"I'm perfectly capable."

He held up a hand. "I know you're capable. In fact I believe you are capable of pretty much anything, Maggie. What I'm getting at is that it's smart to have help. Since I'm already here, I'll tag along."

"Don't you have things planned for today?"

"Chuck and I were going to the drive-in tonight. That's pretty much it for my social calendar."

"What about the hardware store?"

"My assistant is in charge."

"Mack?"

"Yeah. The worst he can do is put everything on sale or buy free muffins for all our customers. I'll survive."

Maggie laughed. "Okay, then, thanks. I'd appreciate the company." She paused and looked at him. "You and Chuck are really going to the drive-in?"

"Lassie marathon. Chuck loves Lassie. Why? You want to come, too?"

"Let's see how this trip goes first. After three hours to Denver and three hours back, in a small truck cab, you might not want to do anything with me except to say 'so long.'"

"You're sort of a pessimist, aren't you?"

"I'm a realist," Maggie said.

"That explains everything." He kicked at a stone on the ground. "You know the difference between a realist and a pessimist?"

"No."

Jake met her gaze. "Not a darn thing."

"Thanks for that bit of morning wisdom."

"Anytime. What say I drive through the mountains and then you can drive in the city?"

"Deal." She pulled her backpack from the basket of the bicycle and handed him the keys.

"Coffee first," Jake announced as he climbed into the truck and started the engine of the big yellow moving truck.

"Um, and Jake?"

He slid sunglasses on his face. "Yes?"

"Thanks for volunteering to drive through the mountains. I was a little nervous about that part."

"Not a problem. I'm a little nervous about driving in the city."

"You, nervous?"

Jake shrugged. "I don't get out of Paradise much these days."

"Do you miss Denver?"

Maggie's glance followed his as he stared toward the mountains in the distance and shook his head.

"I guess not," she answered for him.

He faced her and smiled. "You okay with being my copilot?"

"Anytime," she said.

"Good to know," Jake replied.

Three hours later Jake released his breath when they pulled up to a row of high-rises that obscured the Denver skyline.

"I forgot how close together things are here in the city," he said.

"Nothing like Paradise, is it?"

"Nope." He glanced out the window and down at the curb. "Are you sure we won't get ticketed in this spot?"

"It's for loading and unloading. We're good."

They hopped out of the truck and stretched before approaching the building.

"Really, that wasn't a bad ride at all," Maggie commented as they got in the elevator and headed up to her parents' condo.

Jake could only grin. "Yeah, only a few surprises."

"Surprises? Such as?"

He grabbed her right hand and held it up. "Orange fingers."

"Puffed cheese balls are delicious."

"Yeah, with zero nutritional value. It's fake food."

She shrugged and hid her hand behind her back.

"You're an agronomist who's into organics and you eat puffed cheese balls and toaster pastries?"

"We all have our weaknesses."

"Do we?"

"Yes."

The elevator doors opened. Maggie stood stiffly without moving.

"Aren't we getting out?" Jake asked.

She turned to him, her face pale. "I should probably warn you about my parents."

"Maggie, honey, I deal with all kinds of Joe Public on a daily basis. I get along with everyone. No worries."

"Are you kidding? I wasn't worried about you. It's them."

He frowned. "What about them?"

"They're very, um...structured."

"I'm structured."

"Maybe that's not the word I'm looking for." She bit her lip.

Jake took her arm and gently tugged her out of the elevator. "Let's go. A couple more hours and we'll be back in Paradise. Besides, I'm actually looking forward to meeting your parents."

She muttered something unintelligible under her breath as they walked down a neatly carpeted hallway to unit twenty-seven and rang the bell.

No sounds emanated from the other side.

Maggie rang the bell to her parents' condo again and turned to Jake with a weak smile. "They aren't home."

He leaned his shoulder against the wall. "Did they know you were coming?"

"Yes. Of course."

"Sort of odd, isn't it?" he commented.

Maggie shook her head. "Not really. This is their passive-aggressive way of showing disapproval."

"What do you want to do?" he asked.

She dipped her hand into her pocket and pulled out a key.

"Well, then let's go in and take care of things."

The door to the condo swung open and Jake followed Maggie inside. The Joneses' home was immaculate, though every surface seemed to be covered with either books or travel artifacts. He'd guess from the artwork, sculptures and various knickknacks that they had indeed traveled the globe.

"Wow," he murmured.

"Yes. Even when I was little, it was like living in a museum."

"Which explains your penchant for minimalism."

"This way," Maggie said with a nod. Her voice was hushed, as though she was in a library.

He followed her down a hallway to the last door. She stopped and he nearly ran into her as they stood at the threshold of a bedroom.

Inside the room drop cloths and paint cans covered one corner. Stacks of boxes occupied the middle of the room, along with an oak rocking chair, a small rolltop desk and an oak bureau. The desk and bureau had been wrapped in packing plastic. Even the twin bed had been broken down and neatly covered with plastic.

"They boxed it all up for you?"

"Yes. That's my folks. Ever efficient." She sagged and slipped down to the polished oak rocking chair that was next to the boxes and lovingly stroked the engraved arms. "This chair was my grandmother's. My mother has the mate to it and she cherishes it as much as I do this one."

"Maggie. You okay?"

Her face crumpled. "Oh, Jake. They packed me up like one of their projects and put me away."

"Naw," he tried to reassure her. "It looks like they were getting ready to paint."

"Jake, you don't know my parents. Do you have any idea why I spent summers in Paradise?"

"So you could experience the great outdoors?"

"No, so they could travel the world without being encumbered by a child. I was an accident, you know. They really didn't want me."

"Maggie, that's not true."

She shook her head firmly. "It's very true. That's why all my life I've lived *their* life. Hoping they'd let me in the inner circle of their family. I've never said it aloud before, because I was afraid what I thought might be true. And it is."

Jake kneeled down next to her and took her hand. He stroked the soft skin, then his gaze moved to her face. Maggie averted her gaze, instead staring at her hand in his.

"Maggie, you have lots of family, and friends, people who care about you in Paradise."

"I know. I know," she murmured. "The Lord has a plan for me. I keep repeating that verse. 'Cast all your cares upon the Lord, for He cares for you.' I keep reminding myself that He cares for me. That's what matters."

"He does. And so do I Maggie."

She nodded slowly.

"Come on. Let's get this stuff out of here and go home."

When Maggie lifted her chin, and he looked directly into her moist pain-filled brown eyes, all he wanted to do was take her in his arms and make it all right.

But she beat him to it. Maggie reached forward and slipped her arms around his neck and hugged him. Surprised, he held very still, and inhaled the intoxicating mixture of the vanilla and cheese balls that was Maggie. For a moment he allowed himself the luxury of enjoying her head on his shoulder.

When she finally eased away from him their gazes connected. This time Jake leaned toward her ever so slowly, until his lips touched hers.

She didn't pull away and once again he was lost in the sweetness of Maggie.

Minutes later Jake rested his forehead against hers.

"Thank you," she whispered. "For understanding."

"Anytime, Maggie. Anytime."

Reluctantly he stood, creating a distance between them. He looked around. "Come on. Let's get this stuff out of here and go home to Paradise."

"I'm ready." She glanced at the furniture. "This is actually all I own that's really mine. My maternal grandmother left me those pieces."

"That dresser and desk look like antiques."

"They are. She owned an antiques store."

"No kidding. Were you close?"

"I only saw her a few times in my life."

"We probably should have brought Beck. That bureau and desk look heavy."

"We have two dollies."

"We do." He picked up a box and so did Maggie. "You are aware that Beck is crushing on you, right?"

"No, he isn't," she said as she followed him to the elevator. "I don't understand why this keeps coming up. First Bitsy and now you. Beck and I are friends."

"Maggie, it scares me to think Bitsy and I agree

on something, but I'm telling you. Guys know this stuff. Beck is seriously crushing on you."

"I haven't done anything. Or encouraged him."

"You can't help that you're a beautiful woman."

Her eyes widened and she inhaled sharply. "Stop or this box might slip out of my arms and land on your foot."

He stood next to her in the elevator unable to hide a grin. His Maggie was back, with fire in her eyes.

"Because I said you were beautiful?" he asked.

"I'm the same person. Just Maggie."

"Just Maggie has to adjust her thinking. The beauty on your inside is now evident on the outside."

She blinked, opened her mouth and then closed it.

Jake continued to smile. Maggie Jones was speechless.

"I've got to stop by my house to feed Chuck before we head over to your place," Jake said.

She gave a small nod, though her eyes remained closed and her head rested against the seat. Maggie was emotionally drained. He couldn't blame her. It was probably a good thing her parents weren't home. He'd have easily given them a rundown on what a wonderful daughter they had, along with several pieces of his mind.

"You awake?" he asked.

"Yes. What time is it anyhow?"

"Four o'clock."

"You made good time," she commented.

"Once we hit the Eisenhower Tunnel it was an easy ride."

A slight smile curved her lips.

"I'm glad you drove in Denver," he admitted. "I'd forgotten how crazy the on-ramps and off-ramps were. Why do they call that one stretch of highway the mousetrap?" Jake asked as he pulled the moving truck up to his house.

"Because you feel like a completely helpless mouse in a maze."

Jake put the parking brake on.

Her eyes slowly opened.

"Are you hungry?" he asked.

"We ran out of cheese balls two hours ago. I'm starving."

"We could have stopped," Jake pointed out.

"I wanted to get home." Maggie opened the truck door and jumped down. Arms on her hips, she rotated her neck and then stretched her back. "Which house is yours?"

He laughed.

Only one home stood on the acre of land, bordered by a green lawn and gravel drive, with a detached garage on one side and a small forest on the other three sides. The two-story log-cabin home looked toward the mountains.

Tall windows graced the front. A wraparound

porch with roughly hewn wood rails surrounded the house.

"This looks like a hunting cabin on steroids."

"My escape from the world."

She followed him into the house, where Chuck enthusiastically greeted them before he shot outside.

"Impressive," Maggie said. "And all leather furniture. This is a total man cave."

"Is it?" Jake looked around the rustic home, assessing it from her eyes.

A stone fireplace, with a chimney that stretched to the ceiling, was the focal point of the room. In front of the hearth on the hardwood floor was a large Southwestern-print rug. Copper ceiling fans, suspended from the wooden beams, whirred gently.

"Okay," he admitted, "maybe it could use some womanly touches. But I absolutely do not allow froufrou."

Maggie laughed. "Froufrou?"

"You know. Doilies. Couches with big peonies. Tiny rugs that serve no purpose. Oh, and lavender potpourri."

"Oh, yeah, that's definitely froufrou. You need a sign on your door. No soliciting or froufrou."

"Want something to drink, smart aleck?" he asked.

"No, thanks, but I'm right behind you. I have to see the kitchen."

From the doorway, Maggie gaped at the room. "I guess you do cook," she finally said.

"Try not to let the stove and refrigerator intimidate you. I had to replace them anyhow, so I went top-of-the-line." He pulled a bag of dog food from a cupboard and filled a stainless steel dog dish.

"You and Susan should chat. You obviously watch the same shows on the Food Network." Maggie ran a hand over the granite countertop.

"I did everything in here myself."

"Good therapy, I imagine."

He gave a short nod.

Oh, yeah. Intuitive woman. She was closer to the truth than she could have realized. Ten years and a lot of praying and thinking. Therapy of sorts, for sure.

"Why do you bother with a landline?" she asked.

"Cell phones can be unreliable in the mountains. I have to be reachable by dispatch 24/7. I've also got a CB radio in my bedroom as a backup."

"Makes sense." She nodded. "Mind if I ask you a personal question?"

"Ask away."

"If your dad is retired, why does he spend so much time in the hardware store?"

Jake laughed. "That's not a personal question. Mack only thinks he's retired. The reality is that he's at the store every single day. Sometimes only for a few hours. He loves the place too much to ever really leave it behind." Jake shrugged. "He doesn't pull a paycheck so I'm not going to point it out to him."

She nodded and then paused, frowning. "Do you hear that?" Maggie asked.

Jake tensed. "Fire horns." He slapped his back pocket. "My phone. I left my phone in the moving truck." He raced outside and Maggie followed.

"Are you on call?" she asked.

"No, but I like to keep an eye on what's going on."

He grabbed the phone from the moving truck and read the text.

"Everything okay?"

"This time it isn't your fault," he muttered.

"What's going on, Jake?"

He exhaled before facing her. "Neighbor called in a fire at your place."

"What? That's Susan's house. That's my new home." She released a slow breath. "I don't understand."

"A metal can is sitting in the middle of your driveway, on fire."

"My driveway? That's crazy." She groaned. "So much for flying under the radar."

"We'll go check it out," Jake said as he texted a message to Duffy.

"Thank you," Maggie breathed.

"Chuck." Jake whistled and the dog appeared. "Mind if Chuck joins us?"

"No. That's fine."

Jake pulled open his door and Chuck jumped in. "Backseat, boy. Seat belt," he said as he started the engine.

"Did Duffy answer you?" she asked.

"Hang on. Update coming." He glanced down at the phone. "It's already been extinguished. I'd better call him and get the details."

Jake jumped from the truck and walked far enough away that Maggie couldn't overhear.

"Duff, what's going on?'

"I'd say it was a prank, Chief. Minimal accelerant and what looks like a fancy remote incendiary device used to ignite. A pretty smart prankster. We have so many new faces in Paradise this time of year, it'll be hard to pin it down to anyone."

"Not too many pranksters in town who could pull that off."

"You have someone in mind?"

"Maybe."

"Maggie isn't home, you know," Duffy said.

"She's with me."

Duffy hooted. "Why am I not surprised? I heard you were leading the pack for Maggie's attentions."

"Cut it out. We're moving her stuff from Denver."

"Does she know about the fire?"

"Oh, yeah."

"So what are you going to tell her?"

"As little as possible."

"Maggie won't stand for that."

"Yeah, I know. But the last thing I need is Maggie trying to figure out who did this on her own. So let's downplay the whole thing. Call it a prank and work with the sheriff to figure it out." He paused. "Oh, and let's do our best to keep Bitsy Harmony out of the loop on this one."

Jake checked the caller ID and grabbed the landline on his desk.

"Commissioner. How can I help you?"

"MacLaughlin, I've got some disturbing paperwork in my hands."

"Oh?"

"You've filed three reports on a Margaret Jones, of Denver, current address Paradise, with fire incidents. All within the last month. The most recent report just Saturday. Do we have an arsonist on our hands?"

Jake's heart pounded at the words. He jumped up from his desk and began to pace with the cordless phone to his ear. "Sir. I know Maggie personally. She is not an arsonist. That was simply bad luck and poor timing. The truck fire wasn't even her fault, and I was with her when the last incident occurred."

"Okay. Okay. I hear you and I trust your judgment, MacLaughlin. But it's imperative that you contain this situation, immediately. I've got constituents to think about and I don't have the luxury of running unopposed."

"Yes, sir."

"We want to be sure there aren't any skeletons in anyone's closet. If the media in Denver get a hold of this on a slow news day, it'll be a three-ring circus."

"Yes, sir," he said as he eased into his chair again.

"So keep a close eye on this woman. A very close eye. And have Sam Lawson run her name for priors and outstanding warrants. Let's stay on top of things as a precaution."

Jake grimaced. "I can do that, sir"

"I'm counting on you, MacLaughlin."

"Yes, sir. Thank you."

Jake leaned back in his chair as he set the phone down. His stomach knotted thinking about the commissioner's request.

There was no way Maggie had outstanding priors or warrants. Okay, he'd admit she could be a little forgetful. He only hoped she didn't have too many parking tickets.

Jake ran a hand over his face. If Maggie ever got wind of this she'd be humiliated and completely over-the-top furious. He wouldn't blame her, either.

A knock on the door interrupted him. "Jacob, you busy?"

"No, Dad, come on in. What's up?"

"I've had another idea for the store." Mack pulled a piece of paper from his pocket before he slid into a chair across from the desk.

"You or Bitsy? Are we paying her a consulting fee?"

"Naw, she does it out of the kindness of her heart."

"Great. So what's the idea?"

Mack cleared his throat and glanced at the paper in his hand. "What about a summer fire-safety day? Promote fire-safety awareness? Good time to reach the tourists, too. We can put all our fire-prevention-related products on sale that day, as well. Fire sale, so to speak."

"Dad, this is a brilliant plan. Let me get an official clearance from the commissioner." Jake leaned forward. "You know, I bet Maggie would like to help. Can Bitsy get Maggie involved?"

"Really?" Mack put a finger in his ear and jiggled it. "Did I hear you right?"

"A good idea is a good idea, Mack."

"Here I was prepared with statistics and all. Thought for sure I was going to have to twist your arm." His father frowned. "You're not humoring me, are you?"

"No. I'm telling you. It really is a great idea.

How does Bitsy want to handle this summer fire-safety day?"

"I hadn't gotten that far. I expected you to shoot me down. I wasn't prepared for a yes. How about if I set up a meeting for all of us?" Mack asked.

"Sure."

"I'll get on it." Mack walked toward the door and then stopped and turned back to Jake. "Son, you feeling all right?"

"Yeah, Dad, why?"

Mack shook his head. "Just checking." He put a hand on the doorknob. "Say, what do you think about having dinner at Bitsy's? Real casual-like. We can talk about this."

"That works for me. Can you check with Maggie?"

"I can do that."

"We better get moving fast," Jake added. "The Fourth of July is only a week away. I'd like to notify the commissioner we have everything in place and plan to roll out the project after the holiday."

"Wow, you sure surprised me on this one. I didn't expect so much enthusiasm. Seemed like lately you've been all work and no play."

"Really? Sorry, if I've been a little tense." The fact that he'd used Duffy's description didn't escape him. Jake took a deep breath. "Dad, we're on the same team here. If I haven't mentioned it, well, since you retired you've done a great job of promoting the store."

"Thanks, son."

The door closed and Jake put his hands behind his head. Who'd have thought Bitsy would solve his problem? It was a great plan, benefitting the department and the citizens of Paradise. Working with Bitsy would keep Maggie out of trouble and it could only help her standing with the school board. It would also keep the town sympathies on her side. After all, you could hardly accuse a woman heading up a fire-safety program of being a fire bug. Could you?

Chapter Ten

"Well, isn't this nice?" Mack said.

"Real nice, Dad," Jake said with a wink to Maggie.

"Is everyone hungry? Because I thought maybe we could eat first, out on the patio," Bitsy commented.

French doors opened to reveal a large stamped cement patio. Jake stood and took in the yard. Small pine trees provided a border without obstructing the west-facing view of the Sangre de Cristo Mountains.

"What an amazing view," Maggie said.

"Isn't it?" his father added. "You should see it at sunset."

Jake frowned, processing the information.

"What are those flowers, Bitsy?" Maggie asked.

Bitsy stepped out to the stone path that weaved through the yard, and Maggie followed. "Columbine there. State flower of Colorado, you know. Those are coneflowers. Prairie zinnia." She pointed to the yellow flower. "Of course the peonies have already finished for the year, but the day lilies keep popping up."

"Who did all this?" Maggie asked.

"I did it myself. Of course it's been a thirty-year work-in-progress."

"It looks like a picture in a magazine," Maggie said.

"How old is the house?" Jake asked.

"Sixty years old," Mack answered at the same time as Bitsy.

The two laughed.

"It was my mother's house," Bitsy added.

The house was a surprise. Jake expected antiques and girly gewgaws everywhere. Instead the decor was French provincial, in soothing shades of cream and blue, decorated very sparsely to make the rooms appear larger.

A timer went off.

"Dinner is ready," Bitsy said.

"May I help with anything, Bitsy?" Maggie asked.

"No, she's got it under control, right, Bitsy?" Mack answered for her.

"I do. Now, Jake and Maggie you sit right there next to each other—gives you a fine view of the garden while we eat. Mack, you're there at the head of the table."

Jake held Maggie's chair for her. From the kitchen the aroma of seared beef filled the air.

"Paradise Valley beef. From the Elliott Ranch," Bitsy announced as she brought a platter of prime rib to the table.

Maggie's eyes widened.

"Not a vegetarian, are you?"

"Oh, no. I'm marveling at your cooking skills. I'm doing well to barbeque a hamburger."

"Wait until you taste my garlic mashed potatoes and spring peas. I like to keep the side dishes simple with a meal like this. The meat is really the star of the show."

Bitsy slid into a chair and took Mack's hand. "Let's pray, then Mack can slice the roast and I'll grab the rolls from the oven. I feel certain that the Lord doesn't want us to eat cold food."

"Jacob, will you do the honors?" his father asked.

"Me?" Jake nearly choked on his water.

"You used to do it all the time growing up."

"Okay, sure, Dad." He took his father's hand and Maggie's and bowed his head. "Lord, thank You for this meal we are about to eat and bless this food to our bodies. Thank You for the fellowship of our friends gathered here today. Amen."

"Mighty nice," Bitsy said as she popped her head up. "Be right back." She turned to Maggie. "Come to think of it, I could use an extra pair of hands to bring food to the table."

"Glad to help." Maggie pushed her chair back and followed Bitsy.

Jake picked up his water glass again. "So, Dad, how close are you and Bitsy?"

"Friends, son. Like you and Maggie. Good friends are the foundation for life, wouldn't you say?"

"Yeah, but that depends on your definition wouldn't you say?"

"What I'd say is that a good friend is someone special who brings happiness into your life, cares for you just the way you are and encourages you to be the best you can be."

"That's a little deeper explanation than I expected," Jake said.

Mack chuckled.

"Look at these yeast rolls," Maggie interrupted as she set the basket on the table. "I need to hang out here more often."

"Yeah, that Bitsy knows how to cook. That's for sure." Mack patted his abdomen.

Everything suddenly slowed down in Jake's mind's eye as he observed the movements around the table. He took the big bowl of tossed garden salad that was passed to him and sat thinking.

His father and Bitsy? Glancing up he couldn't miss the adoration in Mack's eyes as he stared at the woman like she was the best thing since peach pie.

He looked over at Maggie. She laughed at

something Mack said, then turned toward him and smiled, her eyes lighting up, her mouth curved sweetly.

Jake's heart clutched. His father's words echoed in his ears. *Someone special who brings happiness into your life, cares for you just the way you are and encourages you to be the best you can be.*

"We need to talk," Bitsy whispered to Maggie. In the other room Mack and Jake debated fishing lures across the table.

Maggie dried a pot and placed it on the counter. "What's going on?"

"I don't want them to hear." She nodded her head toward the dining room.

"Can't you give them something to do?" Maggie asked.

"Brilliant, Maggie." Bitsy turned and called out,

"Mack?" Bitsy called out.

A moment later Mack MacLaughlin stood in the doorway, looking very much like he ate more than he should have and was pleased about it. "What's up?"

"Can you do me a favor, please?"

"Sure. Anything you want."

"There are ten bags of sphagnum peat in the garage. Can you put it in Jake's truck? For Maggie?"

"Ten bags?" He groaned.

"Yes, please."

"Come on, Jake. You heard the lady."

"Sounds like we're working for our supper."

"By the time you're done, we'll be ready to sit down with pie and discuss that summer fire-safety day.

"Then we better hurry, Mack," Jake returned.

Bitsy dried her hands. "Jake sent a request to the sheriff's office to run a background check on you."

Maggie's mouth nearly dropped open. "Me? Why?"

"Shh. They'll hear you. Now, don't get all riled up. I happened to hear the conversation between him and Sam."

"For once I'm grateful you have superpowers, Bitsy."

Bitsy laughed. "I shouldn't be laughing. This really isn't a laughing matter. The fire commissioner is worried about the upcoming elections."

"I've gotten Jake in trouble, haven't I?"

"Jake defended you to the hilt."

"Wait a minute. I don't understand. Jake's running unopposed."

Bitsy shrugged. "Doesn't matter. Too many fires makes the commissioner look bad and he's not running unopposed. Big bucks are on the line in his campaign."

Distressed, Maggie stared out the window.

"We need to find out who started that fire in your driveway," Bitsy said.

She met Bitsy's gaze. "You know who it was, don't you?"

"I can guess."

"Beck Hollander," Maggie said, despair lacing her voice.

Bitsy nodded. "I pestered Duffy until he gave me the details. Beck is the only one in this town who could have created a remote-control device like that."

"It kills me to think Beck would do such a thing. He isn't a prankster and I really thought we were friends." She shook her head. "Why would he do that?"

"Oh, probably because he's jealous of Jake."

"That's ridiculous. Maybe I should talk to him," Maggie said.

"No." Bitsy put a hand on Maggie's arm. "Not yet. Let Sam and Jake finish the investigation. In the meantime, you need to keep a low profile."

"How low is a low profile?"

"Disappear. Keep out of downtown Paradise and the shop if you can."

"That should be easier now that my Uncle Bob is back. I've turned everything over to him and I'm working in the yard until school starts. The only other thing on my agenda is this summer fire-safety project."

"Good. In the meantime, I'll be on top of things. So don't worry."

But she was worried. Jake loved his job as fire chief. Whether he wanted to admit it or not, moving from the city to the small town of Paradise and becoming chief was his self-ordained penance after his wife died.

What would he do if he had to step down?

Maggie's mind raced. This was all her fault. What was she going to do about it? For starters, distancing herself from Jake was the best thing she could do for him.

Too bad, because she really enjoyed their time together. Lately she found herself listening for his familiar footsteps to come through the door of the shop.

Yes. She'd gotten very used to having Jake around. Doing things with him was much more fun than doing anything alone.

Jake would be a hard habit to break.

"My father and Bitsy," Jake said as he pulled on his seat belt.

"Sweet, aren't they?" Maggie mused.

"You knew?"

"It was an obvious observation."

"How did I miss that obvious observation?"

"Maybe you didn't want to see what was going on?"

"No. I think my father was keeping his relationship with Bitsy from me."

"Well, he isn't now. They seem very comfortable together."

"*Comfortable.* Interesting word choice. They do, but I'm still trying to understand how this happened. They have nothing in common."

"Jake, sometimes the commonality in a relationship is simply the same belief system and willingness to respect that the other person is different."

"You really believe that?"

"Yes. You and I are friends and on the outside it would appear we have nothing in common."

"You sound like Duffy."

Maggie's brows knit. "I'm not sure how to take that. Anyhow, all I'm saying is that I think it's nice that they're such good friends. It's obvious that Mack and Bitsy care for each other. They make each other happy, too."

Jake straightened at her words.

"What's wrong?" Maggie asked.

"Not a thing." He shook his head, bemused. "You know, Mack came to me a few weeks back. He said he was going to propose, but wouldn't tell me who."

"I think he's trying to get you to like Bitsy, first."

"As if I were still a kid."

"He loves you, Jake."

"I know," he conceded. "The thing is I don't really dislike Bitsy. She's just too much like me, to tell you the truth. My dad is easygoing and Bitsy, well, she's..."

"Stubborn, headstrong, opinionated, determined."

"Okay, you can stop now. I get the drift."

Maggie laughed. "You two *are* a lot alike, you're right. It's no wonder you butt heads so often."

"That we do." Jake started the truck. "Anyhow, we got a lot done today, though. I give Bitsy credit for that."

"Yes, but we've still got to find a volunteer to go door to door and pass out those refrigerator magnets she's ordering."

"Oh, I've got someone in mind."

"Who?"

"I'll tell you after I seal the deal."

"That sounds a little cryptic."

Jake only smiled.

He waved to a few pedestrians as they drove down Main Street toward her house.

"July means a big barbecue and celebration out at the Elliott Ranch," he commented "This year it happens to land on the Fourth. They invite the entire town."

"Deep pockets, huh?"

"Hollis Elliott has one of the biggest ranches in the valley. The invitation was in the Sunday

Paradise Gazette. They have a full-page ad. Did you see it?"

"I'm trying to stay away from the newspaper."

Jake grinned. "I understand, but keep in mind that this is one party not to miss. I'll swing by and pick you up."

"I'm not so sure I'm going to attend."

"Why not? Maggie, you're a citizen of Paradise now. This is almost your civic duty."

She released a small laugh. "Right. Like going to the Founder's Day supper with the chief?"

Jake's eyes lit up with amusement. "Yes. Just like that."

"I'll think about it."

"Maggie—"

"Jake."

"Okay, but think about the fact that I really want you to go."

"Jake, you're being great about helping me keep all those enthusiastic suitors at bay, but—"

"Uh-oh, here it comes," he muttered.

"Maybe we should talk about where we go from here."

He turned his head and stared at her from across the seat of the pickup truck. "Maggie, don't go overthinking things. All I'm saying is I enjoy your company."

"As I do yours. But this isn't real."

"What isn't real? Those kisses we shared?"

Her eyes widened. Of course Jake would go there. Maggie's face warmed at his words.

She cleared her throat and gathered her composure. "I'm simply saying that maybe we should remember that you've been gallantly helping me out these past days."

Jake's face hardened and he pinned her with his gaze. "Maggie, I'm not aiming for gallant. Maybe you should consider that I don't do anything unless I want to."

Maggie turned her head away, alarmed at his words. Jake might believe those words now, but he'd regret them eventually when he realized that she was threatening his very career.

Going to the barbeque with him wasn't a smart idea. No, she'd stay home instead and work out her frustrations mulching the ten bags of sphagnum peat Bitsy had provided her instead, while wishing she was the kind of woman a man like Jake deserved.

Chapter Eleven

Trouble in Paradise. Jake smelled it in the air the minute he walked into the hardware store. Mack greeted him at the door, clipboard in hand, and followed him to the office.

"Okay, let me have it," he told his father as he booted up his computer and flipped on the monitor.

"Someone spray-painted graffiti on the back of the store. Way up high. Can't reach it with the ladder. Coincidentally, we're missing six cans of spray paint."

"Nice of them to use our paint. Call the security company and have them run the video footage. Maybe we can find our minor-league criminal." Jake paused. "I'm wondering how they got up so high"

"No clue."

"Can you rent a cherry picker?"

"I'll check on that," Mack said.

"Tourist season. You gotta love it," Jake muttered.

He walked over to the coffeepot and eyed the carafe, and then leaned over and sniffed. Mocha vanilla, Irish crème, hazelnut something. Just as he suspected. Bitsy had his father drinking that flavored stuff again.

"Dad, I thought we agreed. No flavored coffee until afternoon. A compromise."

"Sorry, son, but Bitsy came by with a new one for me to try. Red-velvet cheesecake."

Jake grimaced and shuddered.

If he hadn't hit the snooze button he could have beat his father in and enjoyed a cup of real java. Jake opened the small refrigerator and grabbed a can of soda.

"Jacob. Soda at nine in the morning?"

"It's diet."

"Did you buy those vitamins Bitsy recommended?"

Jake slowly straightened and turned to his father. He opened his mouth, thought better of it and clamped his lips together.

Popping open the can, he downed the contents with relish. "Anything else?" he asked, referring to the clipboard, not the vitamins.

"Yes. You have a meeting with the sheriff in thirty minutes about some top-secret fire issue. He refused to tell me what's going on. Oh, and one of the cashiers wants to take a week off to go fishing. Need your approval." Mack thrust a pink PTO form at him.

Maybe he should consider going fishing. He'd already paid for the license. He set the form on the counter and scrawled his name.

There was a silence in the office as Jake read his mail. Looking up, Jake realized his father was still staring at him, a firm set to his jaw.

"Something else?"

"Sally-Anne called and left a message. She wants you to come over for dinner Friday night. She claims she called last week, too." Mack scratched his head. "I can't say I recall that."

Jake looked at this father. He nearly laughed out loud. If Sally-Anne had called last week, too, his father had torn up the message. Jake was grateful so he sure wasn't going to call Mack out on that one.

"Why would Sally-Anne call and invite me to dinner all of a sudden?"

"Got me." Mack stared at him with a disapproving frown. "Thought she gave up on you years ago. Unless..."

"What?" Jake wished he could bite back the word. He shouldn't have opened that gate. Knew it as sure as he knew the sun was going to set tonight.

"Are you encouraging Sally-Anne? That way lies nothing but drama, son," Mack continued.

"Oh, for Pete's sake, I'm not encouraging her."

"Sounds like it to me. Or why would she call?"

"Dad. I'm nearly forty years old, not fourteen. I think I can handle my personal life." He glared at the coffeepot. "I'm heading out to Patty Jo's for a real coffee and then to that meeting with Sam."

He shoved through the double glass doors and fished in his pocket. The keys were on his desk. Terrific. Well, he'd just have to walk, because he sure wasn't going back in there until he had a few cups of coffee under his belt. He needed to burn off this nagging irritation and ominous feeling that something was about to blow wide open.

Jake released a breath and slowed his stride. Maybe if he'd spent a little more time in prayer this morning. He was as guilty as the next guy of talking, praying and not actually stopping on occasion to listen. Just in case God had something He wanted to say.

He sincerely hoped that it wasn't a serious omission and God would give him some sort of wisdom on how to deal with everything that came his way today.

Looking up, he saw Maggie down the street. If he continued on his walk to the sheriff's department, they'd pass each other. He could use a dose of Maggie Jones sunshine this morning. Besides, after their strange conversation as they left Bitsy's, maybe it would be good to touch base.

Maggie gave a friendly wave, and then suddenly turned and walked in the other direction.

That was odd. Maybe he'd call her later and ask her to dinner. Then he could honestly tell Sally-Anne he had plans.

Great idea. The more he thought about it, the more he was certain Maggie was the best cure for a lousy day.

"Oh, Jake, I'm sorry. I have the Ladies Auxiliary tonight."

"I thought they met on Wednesdays." Phone in hand, he glanced at the calendar on his desk.

"It's a special session at Bitsy's house for your summer fire-safety day. The women are really getting behind this idea full force."

"Okay, sure, yeah. I get it. Great that they're so enthusiastic. What about tomorrow night?" he asked.

"You know, I'm pretty busy all this week. But I will see you next week when we meet with your father and Bitsy again."

"Next week. So you aren't going to the party at the Elliott Ranch, either?"

"I've got so much planting and bee work to do."

"Bee work?"

"Yes. My hives."

"Your hives. Don't know how I forgot about them."

The line was silent for a moment.

"Are we okay, Maggie?"

"I consider you one of my closest friends. Of course we're okay."

"Friends. Right." He was starting to really dislike that word.

"Um, Jake, when exactly is your election?"

"Not until November." He flipped the pages on the calendar. "Four months."

"November," Maggie murmured. "That seems a long way off."

"It is a long way off. Why do you ask?'

"Just curious." She sighed.

"Are you sure everything is all right, Maggie?"

"I'm great. Why?"

"You seem a little off today."

"Oh, no. I'm fine. Couldn't be better."

"So I guess I'll see you around."

"Paradise is a small town and we have summer fire-safety day coming up," she practically chirped.

"Can't wait."

He put down the phone. Despite her reassuring words, his gut told him something was definitely off. He had a wild hunch that if he dug a little deeper, his intuition would point straight to Bitsy Harmony. There was absolutely no doubt in his mind that she was behind whatever was going on with Maggie.

The only good news so far today was that Sam's background check on Maggie came up empty. Not even a parking ticket in her DMV report. Guilt had addled Jake for hours after he'd asked Sam to run the report.

Truth be told, he hadn't been absolutely certain Maggie didn't have something strange in her background. Some friend he was. She was an upstanding citizen and he'd doubted her.

Jake glanced at the clock and picked up the phone. What he needed was to get out of town. A little time and space might provide the perspective he so badly needed. And he could use a sympathetic ear to join him. Sam Lawson was the first name that came to mind.

"Sheriff's department, administrative assistant Bitsy Harmony speaking. How may I direct your call?"

"Bitsy, it's Jake. Is Sam around?"

"Yes, Chief, I'll transfer you."

Jake waited a second and then Sam came on the line. "What's up, Jake?"

"Let's go fishing."

There was silence on the other end of the line.

"Sam, you there?"

"Call me on my cell in a minute," Sam said.

Jake disconnected, waited and redialed Sam's direct number.

"Bitsy listening in?" Jake asked.

"Always. I'm in my truck. She's had her ear to the ground and her fingers in my business all week. I don't know why, but it must be something big. Your timing is perfect. I sure could use a break. I'll call my deputy. He can cover today. I'm off tomorrow and Sunday."

"I'll pack the food. You get the bait."

"Can we get the cabin on Paradise Lake?" Sam asked.

"I called Bob Jones. It's ours."

"Duffy coming?"

"No. He's got a crush on Maggie. I don't want to spend my fishing time hearing him moon over her. I asked you because you're not half in love with her like everyone else in this town."

Sam laughed. "So I'm the only one without the good sense to fall for the woman you're in love with? I'm not sure if you've given me a compliment or an insult."

"I'm not in love with Maggie."

"You just keep telling yourself that." Sam laughed again. "I'll see you at the cabin."

Jake relaxed in his chair. Finally, things were under control again. Like the way they used to be.

He grinned, pleased with himself and eager for a break from his responsibilities. It was time for his life to go back to the way it was. Maybe this break would help keep one Maggie Jones off his mind and out of his heart.

Chapter Twelve

What happened? Four weeks ago she'd arrived in Paradise to start over. Now everything was all messed up. Jake, her parents, Beck.

Maggie gave the nearest bag of peat moss a vengeful kick. It burst open, spewing its contents into the air. Grabbing a rake, she spread the peat moss over the garden.

There wasn't a thing she could do right now about Jake and her parents, except pray, but Beck… It was nearly eight o'clock on a Saturday evening. She'd bet he was home. She could and would deal with him.

She washed her hands and tossed on clean clothes. Ten minutes later she was on her bike, pedaling with determination down the street.

A car. She needed a car and soon. Transporting flowers and plants in the basket was becoming ridiculous. Maybe Mack could give her a lead on a vehicle.

She turned her head toward Mack's house, but it was dark. He was no doubt at Bitsy's enjoying dinner. Maggie easily admitted that she was envious of their relationship. The easy friendship and affection.

Behind Mack's little house, the sun had barely begun to set, providing a brilliant palate of orange and red against a silhouette of clouds. The fading blue sky still managed to peek through.

Maggie froze. A dark cloud moved quickly, winding through the sky.

Smoke. Not a cloud.

Was that smoke coming from the back of Mack's house? It sure was.

She jumped off her bike and let it crash to the cement as she ran up to the door and banged. "Mack?"

Maggie stepped back to assess the continuing trail of smoke. Yes. From the house and becoming thicker and darker. She was not imagining this.

Reaching for her cell, she hit 9-1-1.

"Nine-one-one. Paradise after-hours emergency dispatch. What is the nature of your emergency?"

"Smoke. Call the Paradise Fire Department. 92 Mulberry Lane. And call Bitsy Harmony." She shoved the phone into her pocket and dashed over to the big picture window, moving around until she finally found an angle that allowed her to peer into the living room through the glass.

Mack was in a chair in the living room, slumped and not moving.

Maggie's heart accelerated. "No, Lord. Not Mack. Help me, please."

She groaned as she picked up an iron lawn chair from the porch and heaved it at the window. The center pane shattered, leaving large shards. Maggie removed her jacket and wrapped it around her hand. She punched at the shards until she had a path into the house.

Jumping through the window, her sneakered foot landed on a piece of glass. She slid across the oak floor, landing face-first against a large piece of furniture. It wobbled precariously.

Maggie shook her head and rolled over onto broken glass. Grabbing a table, she stood and leaned against the wall until she had her balance back.

"Grace under pressure, Maggie. Way to go."

Heat licked her face. Heat, but no visible flames. Good.

The entrance to the kitchen had become thick with smoke, obliterating her field of vision past the dining room table.

"Mack." She jostled him. "Mack," she screamed. He barely moved, his eyelids flickering in response. Maggie checked for a pulse in his neck.

Strong. Thank You, Lord.

The looming smoke inched closer.

Maggie coughed and tucked her head down and away from the smoke. "We have to get out. Now, Mack."

She unlocked the front door and propped open the screen. Frantic, she glanced around, spotting a large quilt on the couch.

She tossed it on the ground and half dragged, half carried Mack from the chair onto the quilt. Fire horns sounded in the distance, followed by sirens.

The Paradise Volunteer Fire Department. Thank you, thank you, thank you.

Engine Number One never sounded so beautiful.

All she had to do was get Mack out of the house.

Give me the strength to do this, Lord.

Drag him. That's all I have to do. A few more inches to the door.

Maggie panted with the effort. Sweat dripped into her eyes, blurring her vision and she wiped it away with a raised shoulder.

The threshold. Just have to get him across that threshold.

"Sorry, Mack. You're going to have a few bruises in the morning. This is a bumpy ride."

"We've got him, Maggie," Duffy said from

behind her. "Grab the ends," he directed two firemen, who lifted Mack away from the house.

"I need a gurney and some oxygen, stat," Duffy yelled.

Around her, the noises of firemen pulling hoses and ladders as they began to attempt to extinguish the fire filled the air.

Maggie blinked away the moisture in her eyes. "Oh, Duffy, thank you for coming so fast."

"Maggie, what happened?"

"I drove by on my bike and saw smoke."

"The window?"

"I broke the glass and jumped into the house."

His eyes popped open as his gaze moved from the window and back to her. With a sweeping glance he assessed her and frowned. "Medic! We've got a laceration. I need another gurney over here," he called out.

"For who?" Maggie asked, glancing around.

"Maggie—" he winced "—you're bleeding all over the place."

The room was dark, the only real illumination coming from a sliver of light visible at the bottom of the door. Maggie blinked, orienting herself. The patient controls rested on the bed, glowing red and green. Next to her an IV pump beeped at intervals, the digits flashing a constant rhythm as the machine counted the drips.

She reached up and touched her face. A bandage covered her right temple. Gingerly moving her fingers lower, she stopped at her right cheekbone and discovered another bandage. The area around that eye was swollen and definitely painful to the touch.

Shifting on the sheets, she grasped the controls, examining them and finally pressing a button to turn on the lights above her bed. Maggie squinted and adjusted to the brightness. Another button and the bed slowly rose, lifting her to a sitting position. She winced at the aches in her ribs where she'd sailed across the floor at Mack's house.

Outside the room voices echoed. Her ears perked. One was a familiar male.

Jake?

Instinctively Maggie began to lift an arm to run a hand through her hair. But which arm?

Her right hand was effectively taped to IV tubing, which connected her to the blue machine next to her bed. It winked, as though enjoying her predicament.

The left hand, while free, had a thick layer of gauze and tape covering the arm from her wrist to her elbow. Resting on a pillow, the arm throbbed with any movement.

She chose the lesser of two evils. Her right arm, though her fingers kept getting caught in the snarls on her head. A tiny piece of glass fell onto the bed and Maggie picked it up and placed it on the over-the-bed table.

Two taps on the door preceded a harried nurse in navy blue scrubs into the room. The young woman slipped in, then rested against the closed door.

"Miss Jones," she said, exasperation lacing her voice. "The chief of the Paradise Volunteer Fire Department is here. I've informed him it is after visiting hours, but he insists upon seeing you right now."

"It's okay, he's a friend. He's not here to take a report or anything."

"Are you sure you want to see him?"

"Yes," Maggie nodded. "Handsome, isn't he?"

The nurse's eyes widened for a moment. When she answered, her voice held a hint of a smile. "Well, yes, but he's also obstinate and impatient."

"True. We better let him in."

"Are you sure? He seems pretty scary."

"Jake?" Maggie laughed. "He's all bark."

"I'll take your word for that." She gave Maggie a doubtful look as she reached for the door. "Be back to take your vital signs in about an hour. Do you need anything for pain?"

"No. But could you tell me why I have this?" Maggie asked, cocking her head toward the IV pump.

"Antibiotics." She pulled a folded paper from her pocket and reviewed it. "The report I got from ER is that the gash on your arm is pretty nasty. You have quite a few stitches under that dressing. The doctors debated about transfusing due to blood loss and decided to pump you with fluids and see if you bounced back on your own."

"So when will you know?"

"We'll draw your blood again in the morning and notify the doctor. However, the fact that you are awake, sitting up and excited to see a handsome fireman tells me that you're a fast healer."

Maggie smiled. "What time is it?"

"Midnight. You came up from ER about an hour ago. We're waiting on the results of the X-ray and scan."

An hour ago? She barely remembered the emergency room. Barely remembered the ambulance. She did remember the fire.

"How's Mack?"

"Mack?" the nurse asked.

"Mack MacLaughlin. Chief MacLaughlin's father. It was his house fire. Was he admitted?"

"Not that I know of and this is a small hospital."

Relieved, Maggie leaned back against the pillows. "Good."

The nurse left and discussion erupted again in the hall, voices rising.

When the door creaked open Jake stuck his head in.

"Jake?" The man who entered looked the antithesis of the Jake MacLaughlin she'd come to know and—yes, she sighed.

Love.

There it was. She couldn't deny the way her heart thumped into overdrive at the mere sight of him. The thought of never seeing him again had haunted her when the smoke poured into Mack's house and she struggled to save herself and Mack.

Jake.

He gave her a lopsided grin. A five-o'clock shadow darkened his face, and his amber eyes were bleary and bloodshot. His short blond hair stuck up at angles, as though he'd run his fingers through it a million times and finally gave up. His rumpled shirt was buttoned wrong and from what she could see, where his jacket didn't cover him, the shirt was half tucked in and half out of his wrinkled blue jeans.

"Good grief, what happened to you?" she asked.

Jake rubbed a hand over his face. He stared at her for moments before answering, assuring himself that she was indeed alive and well.

Finally his breathing slowed and his heart rate returned to normal. He slowly shook his head.

Leave it to Maggie to try to turn the tables on him again. He bit back the answer that came to him.

You. You're what's happened to me, Maggie.

Instead he said, "Me? Look at you. Duffy said you were playing Superman. Did you really dive through a plate-glass window?"

"I have no idea what plate glass is," she said. "I reacted. That's all."

Maggie was every bit as pale as the white sheets and hospital gown she wore. Her hair was a tangled mess around her face. But there had been no mistaking the pleasure in her eyes when he'd walked into the room.

Yeah, he was glad to see her, too. Relief had slammed into him like a fire truck, the moment he realized she was, indeed, okay.

Jake shook his head. He should have never left to go fishing. So much for his plan to keep Maggie out of his life and his heart.

Their eyes met and he flinched at the blue-and-purple bruise and the swelling that decorated her right eye and cheekbone. She'd be sporting that shiner for at least a week or two.

"Is there a place on you that isn't bruised or bandaged?"

"You're exaggerating."

"No, I'm not. And according to the report I got from Sam, you're a hero." He walked closer to her bed. "You saved my father's life."

Her eyes widened at his words.

Jake stared hard at Maggie. He'd never for the rest of his life be able to forget the moment he got the call from Bitsy informing him about the fire. He'd quickly called Duffy and managed to impatiently interrupt him several times to get to the important facts on Maggie and his father.

She saw the smoke as she biked by his father's house. How had she managed to single-handedly pull an unconscious man out of the house?

He shook his head. Maggie has two left feet, so naturally she fell while doing it, cutting herself on the glass from the window she'd broken to get in the house in the first place.

As he'd listened to Duffy, Jake realized one thing. Maggie Jones meant much more to him than he ever planned. More than he could quite comprehend.

More than he was prepared for.

He paced back and forth at the foot of her bed. Hospitals. They plain made him nervous.

"Have you seen your father?"

"Huh?" The question pulled him from his silent reverie.

"Your father?" she asked again.

"Bitsy is with my dad. They gave him a couple of respiratory therapy treatments and released him. He's at my house."

"Good." Maggie breathed her relief aloud. "What caused the fire? Do they know?"

Jake continued to pace, hands thrust into his pockets, trying to recall the conversation he'd had with Bitsy.

"Jake."

He stopped and jerked his head toward her. "What caused the fire?"

"Dryer vent caught on fire." Jake approached the bed and looked around, looking at everything except the woman in the bed.

"Sit down, Jake." Maggie repeated the words, her voice gentle and soothing.

He sat down on the edge of the mattress. Then he got up. Then he sat down again. After a moment he relaxed, head bowed, and let out a breath of air. "Don't ever do that to me again."

It startled him when her hand touched his arm in a gentle caress of comfort. He should be comforting her.

Jake lifted his head and stared at Maggie before finally making an admission. "I want to hold you but I'm afraid I'll hurt you."

"It's okay." She dropped her hand to his, gripping tightly. "I'm sorry I made you worry."

This time his slow silent inspection dared to examine her more closely, first one arm then the other, then her face and scalp. He looked deep into her eyes. What he saw there shook him to his core.

Maggie Jones wore her heart in her eyes.

Finally, his gaze moved beyond her and to another place, another time. Another woman he'd loved. Could he risk his heart like this all over again?

"Have you got a comb?" she asked.

"A comb?" He blinked and looked at her blankly. "A comb?"

Maggie nodded.

"I'll ask the nurse."

A moment later he returned, triumphant, a black comb and a large white towel in his hands. The nurse he'd argued with earlier practically thrust them at him, when he'd asked. She seemed delighted to have him go away.

He'd apologize to her tomorrow for his gruffness. Maybe have Bitsy bring all the staff pies. Tonight he wasn't himself, that was for sure.

"Seems like a strange time to be concerned about combing your hair."

"This isn't about vanity, it's about comfort."

When Maggie held out her hand for the comb he shook his head. "I'll do it. You can't reach with both your arms tied up." He gently lifted her hair and placed the towel around her shoulders. She stiffened for a moment.

"Does it hurt?"

"A bit."

"I'm sorry."

"It's not you. I have aches in places I didn't know existed."

"You dragged a one-hundred-and-eighty-pound man from the house to the front porch. You ought to hurt."

"Pure adrenaline. Unfortunately he's going to hurt tomorrow, too."

"Mack is from sturdy stock. He'll be fine." Jake looked at Maggie's head. "You've got glass in your hair. Why didn't the nurses take care of this?" he growled.

"I've only been in the room an hour. I've been asleep until now. Then you arrived."

Jake grunted and starting working, combing carefully near her scalp. He dropped a few small shards onto the over-the-bed table.

Maggie closed her eyes as he fingered through the strands. He worked with a quiet precision, moving slowly to remove glass, then combing, all the time lost in thought.

An angry tension simmered beneath the surface of his being as he considered just how precious life was. At times he couldn't understand any of it. Nor could he do anything to change things.

Maggie's voice broke through his conflict.

"Are you going to lose your job?"

"What are you talking about?" he asked, going around the bed to finish the other side of her head. "Why would I lose my job?"

"Another fire that lists me in the incident report. The commissioner. Are you going to lose your job?"

Jake fumed at her words. "Who told you about that?"

She shrugged.

"I know who told you." He frowned. "Once

again, this explains a lot. That's why I got the cold shoulder. Right? You were trying to protect me."

Maggie looked away.

Carefully, he rolled up the towel and placed it on the bureau. "All done. Sally-Anne and the Emporium don't have to worry about me stealing their business."

He offered a rueful grin while looking at the disarray he'd created. "But it sure beats sleeping on glass."

Maggie touched her head, running her fingers through the strands, shoving them into a semblance of order.

"Much better." She sighed. "Thank you, but you didn't answer my question."

"My job is secure. You are a hero. Remember that." Jake stood next to the bed, hands stuffed in his back pockets. He cleared his throat. "There'll be plenty of time for talking later. I mean that. We will talk, Maggie. As soon as you're out of here."

"Will we?"

"Yeah."

"Thanks for the warning."

"No problem. Thought I'd give you a little time to get your strength back."

She raised a brow.

"Quit thinking. Maybe you should try to get some sleep now."

"What about you?" she asked.

He dragged a large, orange vinyl hospital-issue chair close to the bed and sank into it. "I'll sit here a while."

"The nurse will make you leave."

He laughed. "Let her try."

Maggie smiled serenely.

Jake gave her a wink as she leaned back against the pillows and closed her eyes. Without thinking, he reached across the blanket to touch Maggie's slim fingers. They warmed him as they curled around his own. His thumb brushed her wrist feeling the pulse strong and bounding. With Maggie's small hand tucked protectively into his he relaxed in the chair and closed his eyes.

If only he could keep her safe always.

Chapter Thirteen

A quick glance around the hospital room confirmed to Maggie that Jake was no longer present. He'd been there at six when the phlebotomist woke her to get a blood sample.

Now he was gone. Disappointment settled in her heart. Already Maggie missed him.

She lifted the cover on the breakfast tray that was in front of her. Rubber pancakes, runny blueberries and a little container of orange juice. She opened the juice, and then pushed the breakfast tray away. She'd kill for hot coffee and muffins or scones from Patti Jo's. In fact she could almost smell them. She must be hallucinating.

The door creaked open and a silver head peeked in.

"Are you awake?"

"Aunt Betty?"

"And company. Come on in, girls."

Maggie's eyes widened as Bitsy held the door

and half of the members of the Paradise Ladies Auxiliary marched into the little hospital room. Standing shoulder-to-shoulder, the gray-haired brigade filled the place.

"Dear me, Maggie. You look like you wrestled with the devil and he won," Bitsy stated.

"Nonsense, Bitsy. Maggie won. The righteous always prevail," Aunt Betty stated.

Maggie smiled at the exchange.

Bitsy stepped forward and placed a white box and a pile of napkins on the over-the-bed table. Aunt Betty added a tall covered container of coffee to the mix.

"Oh, Bitsy. Is it?"

Bitsy reached into the box and pulled out a few pastries.

"Chocolate scones. How did you know?"

The older woman carefully placed one between the fingers of Maggie's right hand. "Julia from the bakery called me this morning. Told me I had to get these to you."

"How did she know what happened?"

"Ha. News spreads fast in Paradise," Bitsy answered. "The phone trees are still ringing." She said a quick prayer of thanksgiving before Maggie bit into the delicacy.

"This is wonderful, absolutely wonderful," Maggie announced, savoring the rich pastry. "I think everyone needs to help me eat them."

"Oh, no, we brought our own," Bitsy announced. Bags rustled as the women settled around the room and joined Maggie.

Maggie fumbled with the lid to the coffee and Aunt Betty reached over and removed the white top. "Can you lift that with those arms?"

"I think so. This coffee smells too good not to try."

She gripped the warm container and lifted it to her lips, eyelids drifting closed as she inhaled the aroma. What a blessing simple pleasures were.

"How are you feeling, Maggie?" Aunt Betty asked.

"Sore. All over. But other than that, okay." Maggie glanced down at her hands, grateful she wasn't burned or worse. Grateful she was right-handed.

"You know you saved Mack's life," Bitsy said.

A general buzz began around the room at that announcement.

Maggie shook her head. "I did what any of you would have done."

"The Lord certainly ordered your steps last night. Why were you out at night on your bicycle?" Bitsy continued.

"Silly, really. I was going to talk to Beck."

"I thought we agreed that I would handle that."

"The more I hang around Paradise, the more stubborn I become, I guess."

"Not to worry. I have that problem under control," Bitsy murmured.

"Is there something I should know?" Aunt Betty asked.

"No, Betty dear, this is one of those situations where ignorance is bliss. Trust me."

"Good. I prefer to defer the problems to you whenever possible. You handle them so well."

Bitsy turned to Maggie. "The bottom line is that Mack and I are plenty grateful you were the vessel the Lord chose to help him last night."

Maggie bowed her head, humbled by the words. Aunt Betty beamed. "You made the newspaper again."

"Not really? How did they manage to get it into the paper already?"

"Stayed up all night, I imagine. I told you, you sell papers. They're calling you a hero. Heroes sell even more papers."

Maggie nearly choked with laughter at the irony. Then she grimaced, clutching her side. "Ouch, that hurt."

"Careful, dear. I hate to mention this, but they called and said that they want to do a feature article on you."

"I'll have to think about that."

"When will they let you come home, Maggie?" one of the women asked.

"I haven't any idea," Maggie answered. "In fact I don't know much of anything except that I have stitches under here and an assortment of bruises all over."

"I've already made inquiries," Bitsy announced. "You have twelve stitches on your arm and two bruised ribs. They are waiting on the results of your blood work to be sure your hemoglobin and hematocrit are normal." She leaned in closer. "That means you lost blood."

The ladies all nodded with fascination.

"The doctor will be making his morning rounds soon. They may want to keep you until tomorrow to watch for side effects of a concussion."

"Oh, do you think she might have Dr. Ben or Sara Rogers as her doctor?" Aunt Betty asked.

"You never know," Bitsy said.

"I'm curious how you got them to give you all that information?" Maggie asked, amazed.

"Official business, of course. I informed the charge nurse that I am the administrative assistant at the Paradise Sheriff's Department and I am gathering investigative information regarding the fire, for the sheriff."

Maggie grinned. Of course. Besides, who would argue with Bitsy?

"It's the truth," Bitsy said. "Sam will be needing that information. The fire department, as well. I'm merely anticipating their needs."

"You anticipate other's needs well, Bitsy. Thank you," Maggie said. She lifted the rest of her scone from the table. "For bringing the pastries, too."

"You're a member of the auxiliary, Maggie, and our friend. We take care of each other. I assured the staff here that you will have plenty of care upon discharge, as well."

It was like having family again. Maggie fought the urge to get weepy over Bitsy's comment.

"We'll be bringing meals to your house once you get home, so you don't have to worry about cooking," Aunt Betty said.

"Thank you," Maggie said. She nearly laughed out loud at the thought of her aunt inspecting her cupboards and finding only bags of cheese puffs and assorted boxes of toaster pastries.

"Where's Jake?" Bitsy asked, lowering her voice.

"He was here last night," Maggie said.

"He should be here now. I spoke to him in passing this morning. Told him we were on our way in," she said.

That would explain Jake's absence, Maggie realized. He wouldn't come within a mile of anything that could even loosely be construed as a meeting of the auxiliary.

Before Bitsy could comment further, a no-nonsense nurse entered the room. Hands on hips, she looked around, a horrified expression on her face.

"The visiting hours don't even begin until ten," she said, examining her watch. "And you can't possibly have this many visitors at one time."

"We are not visitors, we are family," Bitsy informed the nurse. She stood ramrod-straight and stepped smack into the nurse's personal space.

The nurse opened her mouth, but Bitsy continued. "Ms. Jones has a very large, and very close, extended family."

"You're all her family?" the nurse asked, narrowing her eyes to inspect each and every one of the women.

Maggie's visitors looked at each other and then to their leader.

"You're new in town, aren't you?" Bitsy asked.

"Yes. How did you know?"

"Everyone in Paradise knows that Betty is Maggie's aunt, and myself and the rest of these ladies are practically family," Bitsy said.

The nurse sputtered.

"However, as it happens we were just leaving." She gave a nod to the other women.

Leave it to Bitsy to have the last word. At her order, the ladies of the Paradise Auxiliary scrambled to gather the remains of their breakfast and began filing past Maggie's bed to say their goodbyes.

"We're going to church, then for a little shopping," Aunt Betty said as she gave Maggie a kiss goodbye. "I'll be back in a while. If they discharge you early today, I'll drive you. Otherwise Susan will take you home later in the day. She'll be here soon."

"Oh, I hate to be a nuisance."

"It's no trouble. You weren't planning to ride home on your bicycle, were you?"

Maggie laughed. "No. Good point."

Bitsy leaned over to plant a kiss on Maggie's forehead. The gesture both surprised and touched Maggie. Bitsy Harmony and Jake MacLaughlin were more alike than they knew. Efficient bulldogs on the outside, and teddy bears on the inside.

With a quick wink Bitsy led the troops into the hall.

Aunt Betty gave a little finger wave and a salute as she marched past Maggie's bed.

"'Bye, Maggie," she called out on her way out the door. "See you at home, later."

Home.

The word flowed over Maggie liked a sweet balm.

Mack's breathing was deep and regular. Jake stood counting his father's respirations as he slept in the big leather chair.

"He refused to nap in the bed," Bitsy said, her hands on her hips as she stared at Mack.

"Like father, like son," Jake said. "Two hardheads."

"Oh, I think you have him beat."

Jake raised a brow at her words.

"Care for some butternut-squash soup? Your

dad's favorite and I made a big batch. Though I will admit that it took me thirty minutes to figure out your newfangled stove."

"Not really hungry," Jake said. "But thank you for the offer."

"When did you eat last?"

"Can't remember."

"Have a seat, and I'm not asking you. I'm telling you."

He sucked in a breath and sat down at the table.

Bitsy placed a mat, a cloth napkin, silverware and a glass of milk in front of him. "Here you go." A bowl of steaming soup and a basket of fresh bread teased his nostrils. His stomach growled in anticipation.

"Butter?" she asked.

"Yes, please."

Jake bowed his head and prayed silently. He reached for a spoon and began to eat.

"Delicious. Did you make the bread?"

"I did."

Head down, avoiding her gaze, he continued eating, hoping that Bitsy would wander into the next room.

No such luck.

"Do you feel better?" she asked minutes later when his spoon hit the bottom of the bowl.

He relaxed his shoulders. "I do. Thank you."

"Glad to hear it, because you're going to need

your strength when you start thinking and finally realize that all of this was your fault."

Stunned, Jake raised his head and blinked. "Excuse me?"

"I said—"

"I heard you," he growled.

"The way I figure it, you're about to do some soul-searching and you'll come to the conclusion that not only are you at fault for not realizing your father doesn't have a clue that dryer vents need to be emptied more often than once a year, but…"

Jake opened his mouth, but Bitsy whipped her palm up into the air faster than he could come up with a sharp retort.

"*But* you are also going to blame yourself for Maggie's injuries. After that, I dare say you'll decide you do a lousy job of protecting those you love and retreat into that fire helmet of yours forever."

"Is that so?" He bit out the words.

She crossed her arms. "Yes. Pretty close I imagine."

Anger flared within him, and he fought for control. "You don't know what you're talking about."

"Prove me wrong, helmet head. I dare you."

He jerked back at the words. "What did you just call me?"

"You heard me."

Jake was speechless, though he searched high and low for an appropriate comeback. The woman didn't mince words and he had no response for her little reverse psychology game, because deep down inside he waged the battle of a lifetime, trying to discern whether he really was at fault.

"Romans 8:1. 'Therefore there is now no condemnation for those who are in Christ Jesus.'"

"Now you're going to preach to me?"

"I'm almost seventy years old. Not a lot of time to waste being nicety-nice. So I'm willing to do whatever it takes to get you to realize that it's time to get on with your life. Because until you get on with your life, Mack can't and won't." She huffed. "And frankly, the two of us are running out of time."

"A little self-serving, aren't you?"

"Maybe, but that's not all I see. I see a man with lots to offer and a bright future, who refuses to allow God to take care of those he loves, who instead, somehow thinks that it's his responsibility."

She pointed a long finger at him. "Setting yourself up for a big fall there, Jake."

Jake closed his eyes and looked away.

"Pride. Pure pride when you think you can do God's job better than He can."

He felt her hand on his shoulder. "I know this will be difficult for you to believe, but I've come to care a good deal about you, Jake. You're a good man. You deserve the best. Think about what I've said, would you?"

Jake nodded.

"Now I have to head over to the hospital. The Paradise Ladies Auxiliary is giving Maggie a hero's welcome home. I've got pies cooling on the porch."

"When is she being discharged?"

Bitsy glanced at her watch. "Anytime now. I'll come back for Mack later and he can hang out with us at Maggie's. Keep an eye on him for me until then, will you?"

"Yeah. Of course. I'm staying home until he's feeling better."

"Good and I left you a pie on the counter."

She gave him a nod and headed out the door.

"Jacob?" his father called out.

"Dad, you're awake? How are you feeling?"

"Fine. Just a little sore."

Jake walked into the living room. "I'll tell Maggie to drag slower next time."

Mack chuckled. "You do that, would you, please?"

Jake grinned, relieved his father was going to be okay.

"How do you suppose a tiny thing like Maggie managed to drag me out the door? I'm gobsmacked every time I think about that."

"Adrenaline and prayer are a pretty potent combination."

"I guess so." Mack looked up at Jake. "Bitsy's right you know, son."

"Yeah, I know, Bitsy's always right, but we're not going to tell her that, are we?"

Mack laughed. "I do occasionally. It keeps me in pies."

"That's not my strategy. I will admit she is right. Today. I'm still going to need a little time to figure out what I'm going to do about it."

"Pray, Jacob. That's what you do when you can't figure out what's next. You pray. Call His name and He's there for you."

"I'll do that, Mack."

"Oh, and I find it helps to get a little padding on the floor before you get down on your knees and repent. But that's just me."

This time Jake laughed. "Good idea. You're pretty smart, Dad. Pretty smart."

Chapter Fourteen

"Mother, she's here," her cousin Susan called out. Susan carefully assisted Maggie from the car to the porch, where Aunt Betty held the screen door open.

"Finally home again. Thank You, Lord." Her aunt stopped to examine Maggie in the shaft of sunlight that streamed into the small foyer. "Oh, my, look at you."

"Lovely purple shade, isn't it?" Maggie laughed.

"I called your folks to let them know what happened, but I had to leave a message," Susan said.

"I think they're on a cruise until school starts," Maggie said.

"I want to give you a big bear hug, Maggie, but I don't want to hurt you," Aunt Betty said.

"Really, I'm fine. I just took a tumble."

"Through a window, as I understand. Rambo style." Uncle Bob appeared in the hallway.

"Uncle Bob!" She smiled.

"Sorry I haven't gotten over here sooner, Maggie. Business in the shop is booming. Beck and I can barely keep up."

Maggie laughed. "That's good, right?"

"Are you kidding? Absolutely and I owe it all to you. Frankly, I was a little shocked when I had a minute to review the receivables payroll, Maggie. You've done more business while I was away than I've done so far this year."

"More good news."

"Yes, it is. But I would like you to consider helping me part-time again, when you're up to it."

"Sure, Uncle Bob." She turned to her aunt. "It smells wonderful in the house, Aunt Betty. What's cooking?"

"Right now, stew, but we've got anything you want, Maggie."

"Have any puffed cheese balls?"

"Maggie, really? You want puffed cheese balls?"

"Let her have them, Betty," Uncle Bob said. "She's a hero. She can eat anything she wants."

"Thanks, Uncle Bob. You're my hero for saying that."

"Mags, you look pale. Let's get you to your room," Susan said.

"I'm fine. I look much worse than I feel."

"Are you in pain?" Aunt Betty asked.

"At the moment, no, not at all. They insisted I take a pain pill for the ride home. It knocked me out. I only hope I didn't snore."

"It was pretty loud," Susan added.

Maggie groaned with mortification.

"Stop that, Susan. She's kidding, Maggie," Aunt Betty assured her.

Susan laughed. "So you're all goofy from the drugs are you, cousin?"

"That's putting it mildly. I am definitely feeling no pain." She took a few wobbly steps forward.

"Lean on me," Susan said, leading her along the hallway.

Maggie nodded and glanced into the kitchen as they moved down the hall. She blinked, then grabbed the doorjamb and stepped back. The pain medication seemed to be causing hallucinations. She was seeing double. And triple.

"Wait." Inching into the small kitchen she heard a gasp, and realized it was her own. Every bit of counter space was filled with foil-and-plastic-wrap-covered dishes. Homemade pies, cakes and cookies were artfully arranged on platters that covered the table. There wasn't an inch of table top to be seen.

"Where did all this come from?" Maggie asked, aghast.

Aunt Betty walked over to the delicacies. "Well, let me see. Ah, strawberry-rhubarb pie from the mayor's wife. Patti Jo's bakery sent cookies and a box of pastries." She bent to examine a large carrot cake. "From your friends at the *Paradise Gazette*."

"Ah, yes. My new friends at the *Paradise Gazette*." She laughed.

"The casseroles are from the good ladies of the auxiliary. Every single one brought a casserole. You've got something for every day of the week for a month."

"One casserole would have done me for a month. Who's going to eat all that?"

"We'll help," Uncle Bob promised, pinching off a piece of pie and popping it into his mouth.

"Yes, there's that," Aunt Betty said, slapping at his hand. "I imagine you'll have a few visitors. What's left we'll stick in here." She walked over to the refrigerator and pulled open the door. "Hmm." Her voice trailed off with a note of confusion.

Maggie peeked over her aunt's shoulder. There was no room in the refrigerator. Susan's double-sized professional stainless steel refrigerator was full. Every shelf had been crammed tight with plastic containers."

"Oh, goodness," Maggie exclaimed.

"Don't you be worrying. Nothing will go to waste. What your guests don't finish we can freeze."

"Guests?" Maggie asked, certain her aunt joked. "What guests?"

"You're a hero, Maggie," her aunt said with a smile. "People have been calling all day. They want to stop by and pay their respects. Some are friends of Mack, who simply want to thank you for your act of bravery. We told everyone to wait until Friday. Give you some time to rest up."

"Really?"

"Yes, really," Susan said. "I brought you a new outfit from the shop. My thank-you present."

"Oh, Susan, that wasn't necessary."

Behind them Uncle Bob reached out to sneak another corner of crust.

"Bob, just cut yourself a proper piece of that pie and stay out of the way," Aunt Betty scolded. She turned to Maggie. "He claims he likes my pie best but he can't keep his hands off hers."

Susan and Maggie exchanged a look as Susan helped Maggie down the hall.

"Bedroom?"

"I'd rather sit in the living room. I feel like I've been in bed for days."

They stopped at the couch. "Lie down?" Susan asked.

Maggie kept her feet on the polished wood floor. "The room spins when I do that. I'll sit here until the medication wears off." She grabbed her comfortable quilt from the back of the old floral sofa and covered her lap.

As she settled against the cushions, she glanced around the room. Red roses sat in a glass vase on the curio table. Another dozen, this time pink, were in full bloom on the mantel. On the coffee table a lovely arrangement of pink and yellow gerbera daisies took center stage.

"What beautiful flowers. Where did they come from?"

"Let me look for the cards." Susan took the card from the pink roses and handed them to Maggie.

"The Paradise Volunteer Fire Department. Duffy signed it. How sweet."

"The red roses are from Mack and Bitsy. Bitsy told me that. No card on those."

"And the daisies?" Maggie asked.

"I don't know. They were here when I got here."

Susan's phone buzzed. "Oops. Be right back."

Maggie sank back against the cushions as her aunt came into the room and adjusted the shade.

"Nice view, if it wasn't raining again. I know we need the water, but my joints are not happy." She massaged her elbows and stuck her hands in her apron pockets as she surveyed the fat drops hitting the window.

"Oh, I nearly forgot." She pulled a folded piece of paper out of her apron. "The *Paradise Gazette* called twice and left a number. I think they're worried the *Four Forks Daily* might scoop them. They want a call back ASAP."

"Thank you." Maggie's fingers played with the edges of the quilt. "No other calls?"

"That would be all," Aunt Betty said, handing Maggie the paper.

Maggie was unable to contain a sigh of disappointment. Somehow she'd hoped Jake might be here when she got home. Or at least he'd have called. Had she imagined his caring response at the hospital?

"What is it, dear?"

"Nothing."

"Come on, now. It can't be nothing if it makes you look so glum."

"I, um—I don't suppose Jake called?"

"Jake? Why didn't you say so? He did, but he didn't say much. Isn't that just like a man?"

"I suppose," Maggie agreed with a false smile. She shifted slightly, her gaze following Aunt Betty around the room as she fussed, rearranging the roses in their vases. "What did he say?" she queried.

"Say?" Her aunt leaned forward to examine the flowers on the mantel. She rearranged the roses and plucked a few limp petals off the blossoms, tucking them in her apron pocket. "You mean Jake? He asked if you were home yet."

"Oh."

"Said he'd call back."

"That's all?"

Giving the question some thought, her aunt paused and pursed her lips. "That's all. Now, I imagine you're hungry."

"Not really."

Aunt Betty waved a hand of dismissal. "I'll bring you a plate. You have to eat if you want that arm to heal." She started toward the kitchen and turned back. "Margaret?"

"Yes?"

"Thank you, dear."

"For what?"

"You saved Mack's life."

Maggie began to protest. Her aunt held up a hand to silence her. "The good Lord was watching over you and Mack that night."

Maggie blinked back emotions and nodded.

"Folks are going to want to thank you, Maggie. I know this is very uncomfortable for you, but it will be over in a few days. Smile and nod. That's all that's required."

"Okay, Aunt Betty. I get it. I can do that if it will make everyone happy."

"It will and in the end, you'll be happy, too. Trust me."

"I do."

"Okay, now rest. I'll give you thirty minutes before I bring you a plate."

As her aunt left the room the daisies caught Maggie's attention again and she leaned forward and spotted a small card hidden in the center of the arrangement. She pulled it out.

The daisies were from Jake. Pleasure warmed her as she read the note.

These reminded me of you. Hope you're feeling better. I'll see you when the crowd thins. Love, Jake.

Love, Jake?

The words filled her spirit and her heart and eased her pain. Maggie rested her head against the cushions and smiled.

Outside Jake's window the rain continued to fall and the unmistakable sound of a kitten crying broke through the night. Chuck barked. He'd heard it, too.

Jake rolled over and retrieved the sheet from the floor. Another restless night. No use trying to sleep. Once the rain eased up he'd go outside and check out the animal he heard.

For now he lay in bed thinking while the rain hit the roof in a rhythmic pattern.

How do you wake up and realize you love someone?

He'd been up since 3:00 a.m. trying to figure that one out.

Boy, had life changed in the last four weeks.

Every single day since the fire seemed to drag.

Now Maggie Jones had become the local heroine.

He longed to stop by but couldn't, not while the place was crawling with visitors. He wasn't going to let his heart bleed in front of an audience.

According to Bitsy, Maggie had a running line of well-wishers. And she would know. When Bitsy wasn't nursing Mack, she was at Maggie's. According to Sam, Bitsy spent more time out at the cottage than she did at her desk. Not that Sam was complaining.

Trouble was she was also calling Jake left and right. The woman was driving him nuts.

Every single day he got a play-by-play on Maggie along with pointed insinuations about what he ought to be doing.

Yesterday had been the humdinger finale to the week, starting off the moment Bitsy stopped by his house to check on Mack.

"I will be leaving right after I make your father dinner," she'd informed him as she rolled up the blinds in his living room with as much of a racket as possible.

Jake had nodded as he'd poured his second cup of coffee. He could have advised her that he was perfectly capable of making dinner, except he hadn't.

His silence led to the loudest harrumph he'd

heard in his life. He'd barely sat down to read his mail when she started again.

"Are you taking your father to his follow-up medical appointment with the pulmonologist?" she'd asked.

"Happy to," he answered, sorting through envelopes.

The landline rang, interrupting her interrogation. Bitsy reached for the phone at the same time he did.

"My phone," he said as he held the receiver to his ear. "Hello? Hey, Mrs. Jones. A party? Friday? I can't promise. Maybe."

A self-satisfied smile lit up Bitsy's face. She knew who was calling and she'd played him. Set him up, so he'd answer the phone. Yes. He'd been had.

"How's Maggie?" He listened as Betty Jones gave him an update. "Tell her I asked about her, will you?"

Bitsy Harmony was doing her best to remind him of Maggie.

He didn't need anyone to remind him of Maggie. Since the fire, not an hour passed that a hundred images didn't flash through his mind.

Maggie with those glasses and ponytail and those burned eggs. Maggie throwing mud at him. A glowing Maggie in that incredible dress at the Founder's Day supper.

Maggie and the puffed cheese balls.

Then his thoughts flashed to last Saturday night in the hospital.

Maggie's dark head against white hospital sheets.

He hated hospitals. He last saw his mother in a hospital. This was different, he reminded himself, punching the pillow under his head. It wasn't an ending.

He had sat in the chair, holding Maggie's hand, watching her sleep for hours, until he knew he had to leave. If she woke up she would clearly see his heart, and he hadn't been prepared to admit anything that night. Jake had steeled his heart ten years ago. He never set out to fall in love again. One slip of a woman comes to town and he'd gone and broken all his rules.

What was he going to do?

How did Maggie feel? That was the real question. She had wanted him to pretend to care. To keep the suitors away. Still, he thought he'd seen something else in her eyes at the hospital.

One way or another he realized it was time to go all in and take a risk. He could only pray that Maggie wouldn't shut him down.

The week dragged. Though Maggie did little more than sleep and rest at first, her aunt and uncle insisted upon checking in on her several times a day. With each passing day the aches and pains were easing a bit. Her ribs were less sore and she'd gotten used to functioning around the assorted bandages.

By the end of the week Maggie started spending a few hours a day on her laptop reviewing the class lessons for the fall.

Her checkup had been this morning and the doctor had released her as mending with no complications.

It was Friday and she'd finally convinced her aunt that after today, they—meaning all the ladies from the auxiliary—could let her fly solo. She'd firmly assured everyone that she would be able to handle things on her own.

Right now, she longed for solitude. All the company of the past week had been a shock. Showering and dressing early each a.m. and holding court, just in case someone stopped by, was a novelty she didn't want to grow accustomed to.

Neighbors mowed her lawn for her and pulled her weeds. They had even watered her flowers.

Yet each day passed without a word from Jake.

Maggie toyed with the idea of going to see him. But she didn't have a car and wasn't sure she was ready to ride her bike yet.

Bitsy dropped by nearly every day. A strange alliance had formed between Bitsy and her aunt. At least that's how Jake would have seen the situation. Knowing Jake, he would have been suspicious.

Maggie found it rather touching. The former baking adversaries spent an awful lot of time in Maggie's kitchen talking and laughing and making pies. The little party they had teased about last Sunday seemed to be a go. Tonight. Maggie noted this from her eavesdropping, a habit she'd cultivated out of self-preservation.

A few people over couldn't hurt. They'd done so much for her that she couldn't deny them a little fun. Then things would die down and her life would get back to normal. She was all for that, and anything that would empty her kitchen of all the food.

Maggie had also found herself getting crankier as the week had worn on. She'd jump when a cell phone rang, be it hers or Bitsy's or her aunt's. Though she heard phones ringing often it was never Jake.

Why didn't he call?

Each day she'd analyzed the words on the note that'd come with the daisies until she was frustrated and irritable. She couldn't concentrate. Her mind kept slipping back to Paradise's fire chief. His gentle touches in the hospital, his tender kiss.

She was more than aware she'd fallen in love with him and how pathetic that was, as well. After all, how silly was it to be in love with the man that everyone else in town was head over heels for?

Of course she was fooling herself, thinking

he could possibly return her feelings. He still had a long way to go before he was ready for a relationship.

Musing, her glance fell to the cheerful vase of daisies that she'd moved to her office.

I remind him of daisies?

Was that a good thing?

Love, Jake.

Hmm, love you like a sister? Love you as a good friend. Oh, then there was the time-honored, love you in the Lord.

She stared blankly at the laptop. Looking out the window she saw the garden and reminisced back to the day they had the mud fight. A smile came to her lips. Again she tried to shake off frustration.

Wandering to the kitchen she found Aunt Betty and Bitsy, with their heads together.

Maggie cleared her throat.

"Maggie dear, we were just talking about you," Aunt Betty said, elbowing Bitsy.

What a surprise. Maggie lifted her brows in mock astonishment.

"It's nearly dinnertime. Why don't you change into that nice outfit that Susan brought by?" her aunt said.

"I could do that, if you tell me how many people you invited for tonight."

"We only invited people you know. Or who know you," Aunt Betty added.

"Tell me this—do we have enough food to feed them?" Maggie asked.

Aunt Betty looked at Bitsy. Their eyes rounded with concern.

"Certainly," Aunt Betty said. "Right, Bitsy?"

"I don't know," Bitsy countered, pulling a pad of paper out of her pocket.

"I told you I should have made more cookies," Aunt Betty told her.

"Well, who's stopping you? Go ahead. I think I'm going to make one more pie."

"I was only kidding," Maggie said.

They didn't hear the doorbell as they rushed around the kitchen.

Maggie got up and slowly walked down the hall to the door. Beck Hollander stood behind the screen, his gaze firmly fixed on his sneakers as usual.

"Beck," Maggie said. "Come on in."

"No. I, ah… Maggie, I came to apologize."

He pushed his glasses up his nose and met her gaze head on. "I did it."

"Did what, Beck?" She wasn't going to make this easy for him.

"When I heard about the fire and all you did, I realized what a jerk I am."

Maggie opened the screen and stepped outside.

Beck looked from her bruised face to her gauze-wrapped arm. "Are you going to be okay?"

She nodded. "The Lord was watching over me for sure."

"I guess so," he mumbled.

The silence between them was punctuated by a thunder clap. Beck glanced at the sky and exhaled deeply.

"You get me, Maggie. I think I got jealous of our friendship when you started hanging out with the chief."

"Beck, there are a lot of folks in Paradise who get you. People like you just the way you are. I'm not the only one. Above all, the Lord loves you. He created you to be unique."

"Yeah?" He studied her as if searching for the truth.

"You don't have to do things like that fire trick to make anyone stand up and see you. And by the way that was a really dangerous thing to do."

"I'm sorry. It was dumb. Really dumb."

She put a hand on his arm. "You know what? It's time for you to recognize how special you are. You have to love yourself unconditionally and demand that of others."

"I'll try." He swallowed, looked at her and then glanced away. "Can you, uh, forgive me?"

"Of course I can. We're friends. Friends care unconditionally. We all make mistakes."

"Does that mean I don't have to go door-to-door with those fire magnets anymore?"

Maggie burst out laughing. "Is that what Jake has you doing?"

He offered a glum nod. "Ms. Harmony gave me a list of stuff to help the auxiliary, too. I'll be working on her list for weeks. Maybe months."

"Paradise accepts you unconditionally, Beck, but the whole sowing and reaping thing isn't going away."

"Bummer."

"Yeah. Though you know, I bet Julia would love to help you."

"You think?"

"Yes. I do." She smiled. "Now come on in and let's have some of Bitsy's pie and you can explain that device you used to me. That was really brilliant."

Beck grinned, his face lighting up. "My ninth-grade science-fair project."

Maggie shook her head as she opened the screen door.

Chapter Fifteen

The phone rang as Jake headed out to the store to pick up supplies for the kitten he'd rescued early this morning

A trip to the vet had given the cat, a female, the all-clear. No microchips indicating she belonged to someone else.

"It's probably for you," he told the peach-colored fur ball as he picked up the phone. The kitten shot him a bored expression from her seat on the sofa.

"Jake? Can you take a call for the fire marshal?"

Bitsy.

"A call? It's Friday after hours and I'm not on duty this weekend. Duffy is." He paused, suspicion rising in the back of his mind. "What kind of call?"

"I know that Duffy is on duty," Bitsy stated. "But I figured you would want to handle this one yourself."

"What are you talking about?" As he spoke, the kitten began to chase Chuck's tail. Chuck tolerated it for a few minutes and then ran out of the room. Jake turned around, trying to distract the little feline who now dangled from the phone cord like a furry aerialist.

"I just had a tip."

"Can you hang on a second?" The phone clattered to the ground as Jake jumped to move a glass of water out of the cat's path of destruction. It had nearly tipped over on one of Mack's books.

"What kind of tip?" He asked as he picked the receiver back up.

"Anonymous."

Anonymous tip, huh? Paradise was fifteen miles of jurisdiction with approximately seventeen hundred citizens, give or take, in the winter and a transient summer population of another five hundred. Somehow it still managed to be a community more tightly knit than your grandmother's shawl. Nothing much in Paradise could be done anonymously.

He'd be willing to bet a month of chocolate-chip cookies, even cinnamon raisin oatmeal, which citizen was behind this so-called anonymous tip.

"There's something going on down on Mulberry Lane."

"Mulberry Lane?"

"Yes."

"Where Maggie lives?" His voice rose an octave.

He tried to listen to Bitsy's response as he dove for a coffee mug before the cat pounced.

"Will you cut that out?"

"Jake MacLaughlin, do not take that tone with me," Bitsy snapped back.

"I wasn't talking to you. I was talking to the cat."

"You don't have a cat."

"You're right," he said, running a hand through his hair. "It's Maggie's cat."

"Maggie's? Maggie doesn't have a cat, either."

"She does now." Jake cleared his throat. "Could you please update me on the situation on Mulberry Lane?"

"I didn't say there was a situation. The report was that there is a ruckus."

"Ruckus?"

"Correct. I thought you might want to check things out."

"Ruckus falls under Sam's jurisdiction. Not mine. I am the fire marshal."

"Ed is on duty and he isn't answering."

"Did you try Sam's cell phone?"

"I thought you might do that."

"Me? He's your boss."

"Fine. Forget it."

"Wait a minute. Wait just a doggone minute,"

Jake said, holding a tight rein on a short fuse. "I'll call Sam, then I'll go out to Mulberry Lane, on your anonymous tip and evaluate for a code violation as the fire marshal. But you, the sheriff and I will be discussing protocol come Monday morning, Ms. Harmony."

"That would be fine, Chief." The phone clicked in his ear.

Jake hung up and shook his head. What was going on? More importantly, what was Bitsy up to this time?

A ruckus out at Maggie's.

What kind of trouble was she into now?

Jake prayed none of it involved matches or an open flame.

He took his good old time getting ready. No need to rush just because Bitsy said so.

Jake drove like a tourist and slowed down even more once he turned onto Maggie's street. He stopped the truck in the middle of the road and simply stared in astonishment.

Bumper-to-bumper automobiles lined the road for a quarter of a mile and filled the long driveway up to Maggie's cottage. At rough count there were at least thirty vehicles. The area looked like a used-car dealership during a fire sale. People were coming and going everywhere.

Jake had the fire-marshal truck and the kitten was in a carrier in the backseat.

Glancing over his shoulder he noted the feline

had finally run out of energy. Curled into a tight ball, she snoozed on top of an olive-drab wool blanket, a paw over her eyes as though to block out the world.

He could relate. There were times he felt exactly the same way. Like right now.

Backing the car down the road after an unsuccessful attempt to find a place to park, he pulled into his father's driveway and rolled down the windows halfway for the benefit of Maggie's new cat. He would walk from there.

First he took a quick look at his father's house. The damage was extensive. Once again it hit home how the Lord had His hand on both Mack and Maggie that night.

He started a slow walk up the street to Maggie's, counting the number of code violations as he went. Double parked. Parked in front of a fire hydrant. Blocking driveways. Cars parked on lawns without authorization.

No way, no how could the Paradise Volunteer Fire Department get through this mess.

Clearly a fire hazard.

Hands in his pockets Jake strolled up to the front door. Glancing up, he inspected the heavy dark clouds, thankful the rain had eased for the time being.

Through the door he could see the entire population of Paradise squeezed into the little house. The noise level confirmed his speculation. When his light knock failed to attract anyone's attention, Jake opened the screen and stepped right in. Edging past several members of the auxiliary who were chatting in the front hall, he noted Maggie's office door was closed, so he aimed for the general direction of the kitchen, squeezing past people as he inched forward. The living room table where Maggie worked on her projects was covered with a bright tablecloth and more food than even this party would be able to consume.

Paradise's deputy greeted him from his position guarding the desserts.

"Nice party, huh?" Ed commented. He was in uniform, a glass of lemonade in one hand and two brownies in the other.

Jake stared in surprise. "Ed, I thought you were on duty, doing the Friday-night Breathalyzer bust."

Ed's face flamed red and he quickly chewed and swallowed. "I am. But, hey, I did a little traffic control downtown earlier. Even busted Junior Lawrence for jaywalking. Now I'm on my dinner break."

"How long has this party been going on?" Jake asked.

"Started a few hours ago. You missed the first wave of folks."

"Did I? That's too bad." Jake frowned. "Where's your patrol car?"

"Off the road, so I don't get blocked in." Ed took another healthy bite of brownie and eyed the table for his next course.

"Interesting parking configuration out there," Jake commented. "What was your plan if we needed to get an emergency vehicle down the lane?"

The lanky deputy squirmed. "I'm working on that, Jake. Give me a chance, would you?"

"Just how long have you been here, Ed?"

Ed glanced at his watch. "Not real long. Glad Bitsy got a hold of you. I told her I'd call you, but she said she'd rather invite you herself."

Jake nodded. His baloney radar was going off and registering well over the legal limit right now. So this was how Bitsy invited him to a party?

From behind someone gently took his arm, tugging him into the kitchen. Susan Jones.

"Stop harassing Ed. He's only following orders."

"Orders? Whose orders?"

"Bitsy's and mine," Betty Jones said as she stood at the stove.

Jake snorted.

"Stew or mystery casserole?" Susan asked, wielding a spatula in front of his face.

"I recommend the stew, Jacob," Mack said.

"Dad. I see you're having fun." His father leaned against the counter in Maggie's kitchen.

"Oh, sure. I love a good party. I'm celebrating tonight."

"Celebrating being alive?" Jake questioned his father.

Mack's face lit up. He pulled Bitsy close and kissed her on the cheek. "That, too, but I asked Bitsy to marry me and she said yes."

"Whoa, Dad. That's great." Jake did his best to not show how stunned he really was. "Congratulations."

"Thanks, son."

He stood and shook his father's hand, and then turned and stared at Bitsy for a moment before embracing her in an awkward hug.

"You look pretty happy, too," Jake said to Susan.

"I just love happy endings," Susan said. "Besides, that means more business for my shop. I'm thinking of expanding to wedding planning."

Betty placed a large, steaming bowl of stew and a side dish of fresh biscuits on the table.

"Is that for me?"

Jake turned. "Duffy?"

"Chief, you made it." Duffy slid into a chair at the table and pulled the bowl close. "I got here early so I wouldn't miss the first round of the buffet. I thought for sure you were going to be a no-show. You're not much of a party person these days, are you?"

"I'm here, aren't I, and who told you I'm not a party person?" he asked.

"Everyone knows that, Chief." Duffy slowly broke a biscuit in half and reached for the butter. "Looks like you're in your element, Mrs. Jones," Duffy said, admiring the meal. "You know, serving an army makes your cheeks glow."

"Oh, stop that sweet talk, you'll get your pick of dessert without it."

Duffy grinned.

The mayor of Paradise popped his head into the room. "Chief. Glad you finally made it to the party."

"I'm here in an official capacity, Mayor."

The mayor blustered and adjusted the collar of his shirt. "Why, so am I. I had to thank our newest citizen for her act of bravery. In fact, the town council has suggested naming her citizen of the year. We'll put a picture of her up on a billboard. Right next to mine."

"Oh, Maggie will love that," Jake mumbled. "Where is she anyhow?"

Bitsy opened the oven and checked a casserole inside. "Maggie is in her office with a reporter from the *Paradise Gazette*."

"What's going on?" Jake asked.

"He's been here for an hour or two getting an interview for a big article that will be in the Sunday *Denver Chronicle* as well as the *Gazette*. Even brought a photographer and all."

She deposited a stack of dirty plates into the sink and turned on the water.

"I thought Maggie was allergic to newspapers."

"Ask her," Bitsy said.

The back door of the kitchen opened and Beck Hollander stepped inside.

"Beck?" Jake said.

Bitsy turned around. "I invited Beck. He's spoken to Maggie already. We set up a meeting to discuss the summer fire-safety day. Beck will be going door-to-door for us per your instructions. In fact, he's promised to work for the auxiliary until school starts. Whatever we need him to do. Right, Beck?"

Beck mumbled and stared at his sneakers.

"Excuse me, son?" She nudged him along.

"Yes, Ms. Harmony."

"Isn't that nice?" Bitsy asked.

"If you run out of things for Beck to do, send him over to the firehouse."

"I'll do that, Jake." Bitsy winked at Jake and grinned, pleased with herself.

Sam Lawson wedged his way into the kitchen.

He glanced from Duffy to Jake and then to the stew. "I thought you said there was a ruckus here. Looks like a party to me. But that can't be. You don't do parties, do you, Jake?"

"Who started that rumor?" Jake muttered.

"A ruckus?" Betty Jones asked.

"I don't see any ruckus here," Mack chimed in.

"I'm not sure," Sam said. "Maybe that wasn't what Jake said that Bitsy said. It was third-party information, which is highly unreliable to start with. It's entirely possible that I might have gotten everything wrong."

Bitsy turned to Jake. "I was simply giving him the report."

"Whose report?" Jake asked.

"I told you it was called in anonymously."

Jake's gaze pinned Bitsy. "You could have just asked me to come over."

"Already tried that." Her expression clearly said he should have been there a week ago.

"I'll have you know that I planned to come out tonight. In fact I brought Maggie something," Jake said.

"Oh?"

"It's in the truck."

Bitsy gave a half smile as she assessed him. "I'm sorry, Jake," she said. "Then I guess I underestimated you."

"Happens often enough around here," he mumbled.

"Ready to eat?" Sam asked.

Jake looked to Sam. "Yeah, let's grab a plate. I'm not seeing any ruckus and if I close my eyes, I don't even see any code violations."

Sam grinned. "I was hoping you'd say that. Ed called me and told me that he'd saved me a brownie."

The door to Maggie's office opened, and all heads turned. The reporter stood back as Maggie walked out.

Maggie never looked so lovely. There was still a small bandage on her temple and she sported a shiner that covered most of the area around her right eye, as Jake had predicted. Her hair floated around her face, causing him to readily remember removing glass from the light brown strands. The long-sleeved blouse she wore hid most of the dressing on her arm.

The reporter said something close to her ear and Maggie laughed; the effect lighting up her face. Without warning, a stab of jealousy sliced though Jake. It was much more painful than he could have ever anticipated.

Maggie had come out of this whole ordeal changed, as evidenced by the peace and confidence she radiated. "Jake," Maggie said, surprise and pleasure in her voice.

"I'll call you, Maggie," the reporter said as he left.

Maggie nodded vaguely, her eyes still on Jake.

Looking at the strapping younger man, Jake suddenly felt very old. Too old to be playing games of the heart. Way too old to be experiencing jealousy.

"Hello, Sam, Duffy," Maggie said. "Sam, you need to grab a plate."

"I agree," Sam said. "Maybe even two."

Maggie laughed. "Multitasking. Good idea. Jake, aren't you going to eat?" she asked.

"You know what? I am hungry," Jake said. "I guess I could hang around a while." He smiled at Maggie, suddenly realizing that once again, Bitsy was right. He should have been here a week ago.

By the time Jake downed his second helping of stew with at least four more biscuits, the first bolts of lightning streaked across the night sky. Bitsy had insisted Maggie sit down and eat with Jake. A wave of exhaustion rolled over her as she pushed back her partially eaten meal.

The guests had made a significant dent in the bounty spread across the counters and three tables. As the sound of thunder boomed overhead, several of her Paradise neighbors had begun to slowly gravitate toward the front door.

It had been a pleasant day, but now as the hours stretched into evening, Maggie found she was more than ready for the party to end. Being an extrovert, even if only for the day, was draining. She hated to admit it, but she wasn't up to par physically yet. She was tired and aching.

What she longed for was to sit on the porch with a cup of tea, relax and listen to the quiet noises of the country.

She said nothing, however, because if the party

ended, Jake would also leave, and for the moment she simply wanted to enjoy his presence.

As though reading her mind, Jake's gaze connected with hers across the kitchen table. When she attempted to hide a yawn, he smiled and winked.

"Bitsy," he said, standing to clear the table.

Bitsy turned from the sink where her hands were immersed in suds.

"Maggie's looking worn-out." He scooped up Maggie's plate as he cleared his own.

Bitsy looked from Jake over to Maggie.

"What do you want me to do, Jake?"

"You could mention that ticketing of the vehicles might commence in thirty minutes."

"Roger that, Chief."

An hour later Maggie sat alone on her porch, tea in hand. Bitsy had done an amazing job of orchestrating the retreat.

The sky truly opened up then and large drops of water pelted the last guest's car as taillights faded into the distance. After a few minutes the rain became steady and rhythmic. Now this was a welcome guest.

A beacon in his yellow rain slicker, Ed gave a final salute to the sheriff as he drove away. Sam backed the patrol car off the lawn and gave a friendly toot of the horn to signal his own departure.

Jake? She didn't even know where his vehicle

was. He had apparently already disappeared. They hadn't even had a chance to talk. Deep disappointment pricked Maggie.

Then she noticed the red fire-marshal truck pull up the drive closer to the house. When its door opened Jake dodged puddles and rain as he raced to the porch, a jacket over his head. He shook the water from his broad form and stood grinning down at her. He'd never looked so good.

"Hi," he said.

"Hi," she returned. "Bitsy sure knows how to clear a room."

"A rare talent, huh?"

Maggie nodded. "For which I am very grateful."

For moments they simply stared at each other.

"Come back for pie?" Maggie asked.

"Oh, something like that."

"Bitsy left me two."

"Two pies?" He looked her up and down. "I get one a year if I am really lucky and this is your third in what? Five weeks? A month? I'm telling you, ever since you hit town the pies have been running fast and loose."

"Must be my winning personality."

He snorted. "Or maybe the bandage on your head, your bruised face and the gauze on your arm."

Maggie glared.

Jake only chuckled. "I need a favor."

"You're supposed to sweeten someone up when you want a favor. Not insult them."

He shook his head and made a sound of disgust. "I'll get it right one of these days."

"What's the favor?" Maggie asked.

Lifting his jacket he revealed a damp bundle of pale orange fur cowering in the crook of his arm.

"A kitten. He's shivering."

"She. Can you keep her?"

"We've already discussed this."

"Is that your final answer?"

Maggie put her cup on the ground and stood, reaching for the kitten. "I don't do cats."

"This is not a cat. It's a kitten."

She shook her head and opened the screen with the animal in her arms. Jake followed.

"Where'd you find her?" Maggie asked, opening the hall closet. She pulled out a fluffy bath towel and gently rubbed the fur dry. The animal stopped shivering and began purring like a small motor.

"In the woods by my house. She's already been to the vet. All that's left is to pick out a name."

"You left her in the truck all this time?"

"In a carrier, nice and warm with the vehicle windows open for ventilation."

"She's terrified."

"The thunder. Mother Nature's fault. Not mine."

She ignored Jake, but was unable to resist rubbing her cheek against the soft fur, and cooing soft words of reassurance.

"So everything is working out nicely, isn't it?" she finally said.

"What are we talking about here?" Jake asked. "The cat?"

"No. People. Mack and Bitsy are getting married. That should get Bitsy out of your hair, right?"

"In my wildest dreams, they take a cruise around the world and come back and move into Bitsy's house. So that would be a yes."

She chuckled. "And Beck admitted to setting that fire and apologized."

"Don't you think you're letting him off easy for arson?"

"You're going to have to trust me, Jake. Beck and I have an understanding. He's not going to act out like this again."

She put her hand on Jake's sleeve. "Besides, he has so much auxiliary service scheduled, he'll think long and hard before he does anything like that again."

"I don't get why he did it in the first place?'

"He was acting out because he thought you were a risk to his friendship with me."

"Am I?" He looked at her.

"I think I can handle more than one friend in my life."

He nodded in agreement. "So what's going

on with your interview? I thought you were less than enthusiastic about the newspaper industry."

"They're printing a big article about the fire with a tie-in focusing on the Paradise Volunteer Fire Department." She smiled, pleased with her plan. "This should guarantee your reelection, Jake."

"You did the interview for me?"

"It seemed only fair, after all, I was the one who got you in trouble."

"Maggie, you didn't have to do that. I wasn't in trouble."

"I wanted to do it. You've done so much for me already."

The kitten crawled up to Maggie's shoulder and licked her face with a quick flick of a pink tongue.

"So what is it I'm supposed to do with this little peach here?" Maggie asked, tugging the kitten back down into her arms.

"She needs a place to stay. Naturally I thought of you and how you're all by yourself here."

"Maybe you missed the part of the discussion where I said I don't like cats."

Jake attempted to level her with a look, but Maggie ignored him and stroked the kitten gently under the chin. Then she put the kitten down to wander around the kitchen.

"Can she stay?" he asked.

"I'll think about it."

"You've changed, Maggie."

"No, I've grown. These weeks in Paradise have been about me uncovering who I am. Me growing into me. Maybe you won't like the real Maggie. Have you ever considered that?"

"I like her fine."

"Then where have you been all week?" she asked softly. Maggie stepped closer to him. Close enough to smell the pine on his clothes and see the truth in his eyes.

He stared at the floor, hands shoved in the pockets of his navy uniform pants. Finally, he began speaking again.

"I was afraid, Maggie. Seeing you in that hospital bed brought back every one of my fears. Memories I've stuffed away for ten long years. My mom's death and Diana's. I didn't know if I could do it again. Risk everything again and maybe lose."

"And now?"

"I love you, Maggie Jones. I've been in love with you since that first fire."

"When I burned the eggs? In that old T-shirt and my hair in a ponytail? And it wasn't a fire. Just smoke."

"Whatever. You were beautiful. That's the picture I'll always carry in my heart. The very first time I saw you."

"I wish you would have told me. It would have saved me a lot of trouble."

"I was fighting my feelings. Self-preservation."

Maggie stopped talking, suddenly letting his words sink in. He loved her.

Pleasure warmed her inside and out. He loved her. But it wasn't enough. She wouldn't stop, wouldn't give in until they'd settled everything. She didn't want anything standing between them.

"The thing is, Jake, you can't move forward if you're going to spend your life worrying about me."

His gaze never left hers, taking in the words. He nodded as she continued.

"Your life has been safe the past ten years. Constant and predictable. Just like mine." She refused to look away from him as she spoke the words.

"That knock on your head sure gave you some insight, huh?" He reached out to take her hand, rubbing his thumb softly over the skin.

"What about you, Maggie? You were pretty emphatic about not looking for a man in your life."

Her glance flew to his face. "I guess I did say that, didn't I?"

"Several times."

"Hmm, I may need to reevaluate my stance."

"That's probably a good idea because you're stuck with me. For life."

Maggie stood very still, hope building in her

heart, yet she was very much afraid she'd misunderstood his words.

"Did you hear me?" he whispered.

She nodded. Her voice became almost a whisper as she spoke the difficult words. "That fire was a wake-up call for me. I almost lost you, Jake. We both almost lost your father."

His eyes widened and she saw the love on his face. While it was almost her undoing, she knew she had to finish.

"I won't let it happen again. I'm glad to be alive, so I can love you in return. I'm glad you love me, but are you ready to step out in faith?"

"Bitsy says I have to let the Lord take care of people I love and stop trying to do it all myself."

"Why do you suppose she's so smart?" Maggie asked.

"I'm not sure, but it's annoying, isn't it?"

Maggie laughed.

Jake wasted no time folding her into his embrace. Maggie rested her head against his heart, listening to the steady beat for minutes. He raised a hand and gently stroked her hair as his chin nuzzled her close.

"You love me?" he asked, releasing her to look deep into her eyes.

"How could I not? But Jake, love isn't enough. We both have to have the courage to take a chance on our future. Turn it over to Him."

"Are you proposing to me?"

Heat rushed to her face as she struggled for a response. Then she laughed. "Maybe I am."

Jake lifted her chin with his finger. "I sure hope so, because this is going to make Mack and Bitsy very happy." He gave her a goofy grin.

"But what about you?" she asked. "Does this make you happy?"

"It does," Jake murmured. "Thanks for returning to Paradise, Maggie."

"Pretty amazing how our paths crossed, isn't it?"

He nodded. "Yeah. Pretty amazing. I love you, Maggie Jones. You're right. It is time to step out in faith."

His mouth touched hers for the sweetest kiss.

When he lifted his head, Maggie looked into his eyes. "Can we make it, Jake?" she asked.

"Are you asking for guarantees? I can't give you that, but I can promise to love you and to listen to the Lord. Oh, and to keep you in cheese puffs and toaster pastries."

Her laughter filled the room.

"So maybe we'll have another few years together." He shrugged. "Maybe we'll have fifty."

"If we don't?"

"Well, at least we'll know we loved each other our very best every single day."

As Maggie stood on her toes to place a kiss on his lips the kitten wedged between them and attempted to crawl up Jake's pant leg.

"Have you noticed your kitten's fur is the exact color of those pies you love so much?" Maggie asked.

"Our cat," he said.

Maggie let out a breath. "Okay, our cat. But absolutely no dogs."

"No dogs," he repeated. "Except Chuck."

"Except Chuck."

He laughed.

"Ready for some pie?" she asked.

"It really doesn't get any better than this, does it, Maggie?" Jake asked, leaning against the refrigerator with the kitten in his arms.

Maggie smiled as she pulled out Bitsy's pie.

Jake MacLaughlin would be easy to love. Faith, pie and kisses. They already had a built-in family, right here in Paradise.

What else could they possibly ask for?

Epilogue

"Maggie." Jake knocked again.

She cracked open the door to the church's bridal dressing room and smiled. His heart began a slow melt and he nearly forgot why he was there in the first place.

"Open the door, sweetheart," he murmured.

"Jake, you aren't supposed to see the bride before the wedding."

"That only applies to the groom. I'm the best man."

"Oh. I suppose you're right."

Before he realized what hit him, Maggie had carefully stepped into the hallway and launched herself at him, slipping her arms around his neck.

Jake's lips met hers and he kissed her.

"Thank you," Maggie said with a sigh when they had parted. "I needed that."

He exhaled deeply and laced his fingers through hers.

"Anytime."

"Did you need something?" she asked.

"Yes. But now I've forgotten what it was."

Maggie laughed.

"You look amazing," Jake said, taking in the cornflower-blue dress with the deep blue sash. "What do they call that material?"

"Chiffon." She twirled around and the bottom of the dress ruffled and swirled with the movement. "But I have to get back in there and help the bride."

He reached for her right hand and kissed the palm, then ran a finger over the engagement ring. "Thank you for agreeing to be my wife."

"Oh, Jake." She swallowed, her voice thick.

"By the way, a package arrived at the fire station today."

"A package?"

"From your parents."

"My parents sent a package to the fire house?"

"Yeah. You should see what's inside."

"What is it?"

"Your rocking chair's matching pair."

Maggie gasped. "What did you do? That chair is pretty much a seal of approval of our engagement. I never thought my mother would part with it."

"Your parents and I had a long-distance chat. I think we're friends now."

"But how?"

"I thanked them for raising such an amazing daughter. Then I began to list all your fine qualities." He shrugged. "I wouldn't shut up. It's possible they gave their approval to shut me up."

Maggie laughed and hugged him again.

Jake nodded toward the bridal-suite door. "How's our bride doing?"

"Very subdued today."

"May I see her?"

Maggie's brows rose in surprise. "Okay, let me see if she's presentable." She opened the door and left him alone in the hall.

Jake paced back and forth along the ruby carpet. "Lord, help me not to mess this up. It's in Your hands."

"Come on in," Maggie called.

Bitsy Harmony stood in the middle of the room in a long-sleeved off-white lace dress. Scoop-necked, it reached her knees. Her hair had been swept into some sort of twist on the top of her head.

She smiled when she saw him in the doorway, her bright blue eyes alert and questioning.

"Jake, you aren't having cold feet about being Mack's best man, are you?"

"Not at all. I'm honored." He reached into his tuxedo jacket and pulled out a small box. "As I understand the tradition, it's something old and something new, something borrowed and something blue."

Bitsy nodded.

"I brought you something new to wear when you marry my father." Jake opened the box. Inside rested a pearl necklace. He'd taken great care to select it from the jeweler in Monte Vista, not wanting his secret to make it to the loose lips of the citizens of Paradise.

A collective sigh rose from Bitsy and Maggie and the other two bridesmaids.

"Oh, Jake," Bitsy murmured. "They're lovely."

"Welcome to the family, Bitsy. Thank you for making my father so happy. I'm praying for a long and happy marriage for you and Mack."

Bitsy sniffed and blinked her eyes rapidly as Jake took the necklace from the box and reached out to put it around her neck. He kissed her soft cheek and released her.

"Thank you, Jake. I'm speechless and I think you, of all people, know how rare that is."

Jake laughed. "Well, then maybe I better take this opportunity to thank you for all the crazy machinations that went on to get Maggie and me together. You know, of course, that I was one step from being in love with her the first time she burned those eggs?" He glanced fondly at Maggie.

"Of course. It was the Lord's plan. I simply hurried things along."

He smiled and glanced at his watch. "I'll leave

you ladies to finish. Fifteen minutes before you become Mrs. Jacob MacLaughlin Senior, Bitsy."

Maggie slipped her arm through his as he headed to the door. Outside the room she placed her arms around his neck once more. "I didn't think it was possible to love you any more than I do, but, Jake MacLaughlin, I do."

"I love you, too, Maggie. I thank God every day for bringing you into my life."

"Me, too." She smiled. "Me, too."

* * * * *

Dear Reader,

Welcome back to Paradise, Colorado. Paradise is a fictional town set in the area of Del Norte, Colorado.

Maggie and Jake's story is the third in the Paradise series and one of my favorites. I like unconventional women and Maggie is definitely that. I so relate to her feeling like a square peg in a round hole. However, as children of God, it's important that we eventually embrace the fact that we are created purposely by Him to be unique. A vessel created for a particular purpose in the Kingdom of God. So let's rejoice in the special abilities and talents He has given us.

In Maggie and Jake's romance, and Bitsy and Mack's, it's that difference, those polar-opposite personality traits, that draws them together. When two people learn to love the differences in each other, a lasting relationship based on respect and honor is created.

I hope you enjoy their story and do drop me a line to let me know. I can be reached at tina@tinaradcliffe.com or through my website, tinaradcliffe.com.

I'd really love to hear from you.

Tina Radcliffe